Also by Jamie Davis

Sapiens Run Trilogy

Book 1 - *Cyber's Change*

coming soon

Book 2 - *Cyber's Underground*

Book 3 - *Cyber's Escape*

—

The Delivery Mage (5 books)

Book 1 - *Deliver or Die*

—

The Broken Throne Series (5 books)

Read book 1 - *The Charm Runner*

—

The Accidental Traveler LitRPG Trilogy

(with C.J. Davis)

Read book 1 - *The Accidental Thief*

—

Accidental Champion Trilogy

(with C.J. Davis)

Read book 1 - *Accidental Duelist*

—

Extreme Medical Services Series (8 books)

Read book 1 - Extreme Medical Services

—

Eldara Sister Series (2 books)

Read book 1 - *The Nightingale's Angel*

—

Follow on Facebook for updates, news, and upcoming book excerpts

Facebook.com/jamiedavisbooks

—

CYBER'S CHANGE

Sapiens Run Book 1

JAMIE DAVIS

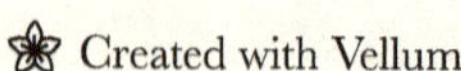 Created with Vellum

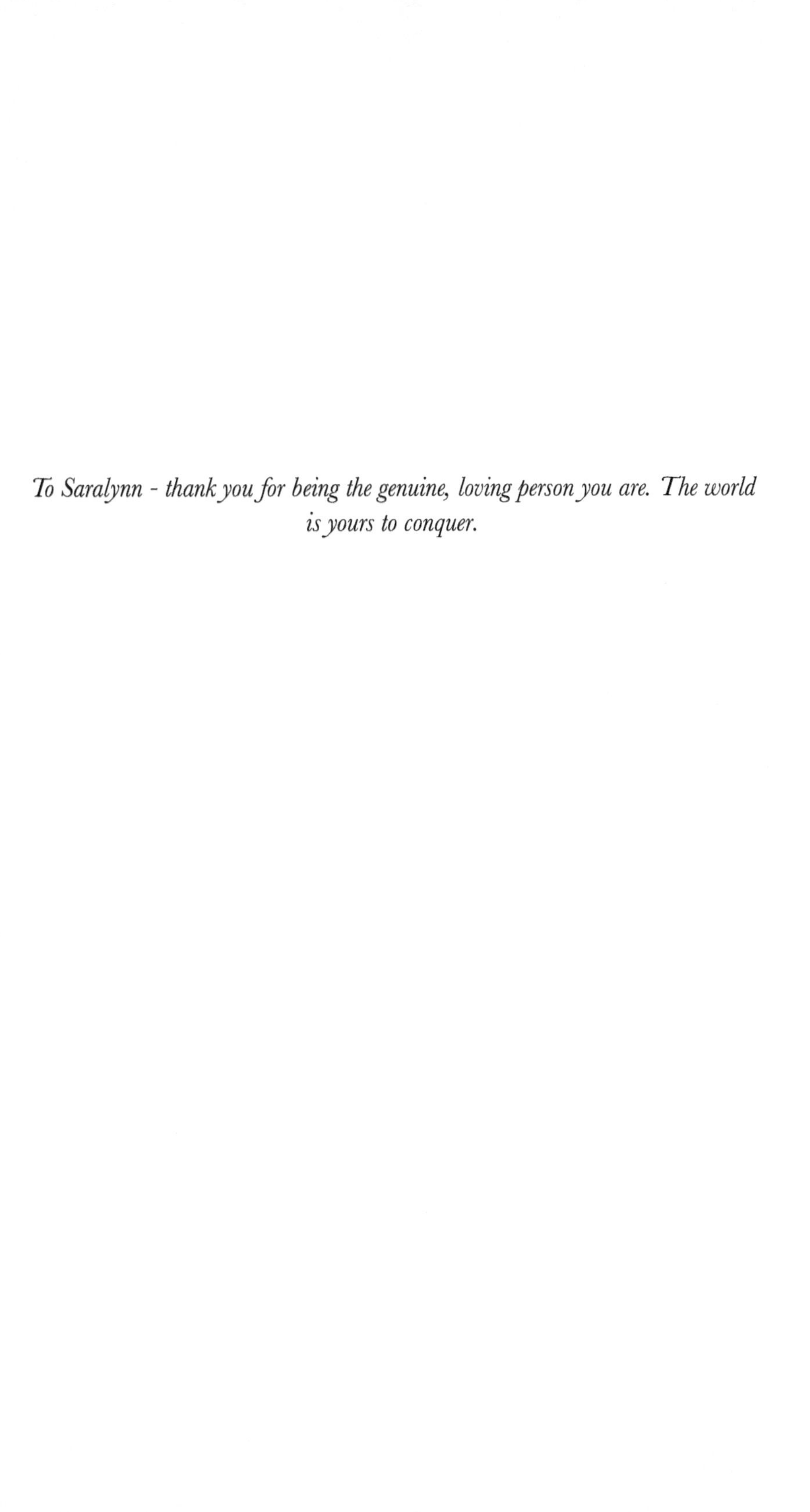

To Saralynn - thank you for being the genuine, loving person you are. The world is yours to conquer.

Chapter 1

CASS ARMSTRONG PICKED up the last stack of T-shirts from the suitcase and placed them in the dresser beside her bed. She put the new one she'd received upon arrival on top of the others. The words "Class of 2054" framed the university logo on the front of the new shirt. Cass slid the drawer shut and flipped the suitcase closed.

"All finished, honey?" Cass's mother Faye asked.

"Yeah, that's the last of it."

"Good, we just have to wait for Daddy to bring up the last box from the car."

Cass's thirteen-year-old sister, Elena, burst into the room from the dormitory hallway. "This place is so supe, Cass. There are so many kinds of people here. They're all so different from us. I can't believe you're going to live here."

"Different's one way to put it," Faye said.

Cass cringed and looked toward the door, scanning to see if any of her new dorm mates overheard the narrow-minded comments from her sister and mother.

Faye continued, unaware of her eldest daughter's pained expression. "I still don't understand why you didn't choose to attend one of the Sapiens-recommended college programs. They're fully accredited and all your friends from home are going to one of them. You know the risks you run when you choose a regular university attended by all these others, Cassie. The people here aren't like us."

"Mom, keep your voice down, please. You know I can't get a degree in political science worth a damn at one of the Sapiens' so-called colleges. I need to go to school here if I'm going to help Daddy with his work."

Faye started to interrupt Cass, but her daughter kept going.

"You don't have to worry about me, Mom. I'm not going to go away to college and come home with all sorts of cyber-enhancements like Maggie did."

"We don't talk about her anymore, Cass. You know that." Her mother shuddered at the mention of her niece.

The tone of her mother's voice stopped Cass. She turned away and straightened her makeup containers on top of the dresser. It was an awkward subject for all of them.

Cass missed Maggie, who was only two years older than herself. The family had disowned both her aunt and her cousin after Maggie returned from college with some embedded electronics and cybernetic skin enhancements. They were relatively minor compared to some, just a few v-tats. They were enhancements nonetheless and Cass's family's leadership position in the Sapiens movement required them to shun that branch of her mother's family.

"I'll be fine, Mom. Promise."

"Promise what?" James Armstrong said, entering the dorm room behind Cass.

She turned and smiled at her father. "Hi, Daddy. It's nothing." She pointed at the box he carried. "Is that the last thing?"

"Yes, finally." He set the plastic bin down on the bed.

It contained all of Cass's newly purchased desk supplies as well as the special-order tablet computer her father bought her for school.

James shook his head and pushed the door closed. He made sure it was latched and scowled as he turned around. "I can't believe all the damned subs there are in this place, Cassie."

"Dad, you can't talk like that," Cass admonished him. "We're not in the middle of the compound. You of all people know better than that. You're the politician after all."

"Yeah, well, that's why I shut the door. I can be as politically correct as the next guy when necessary but I'm still a little pissed off that my daughter is going to be living near so many people pretending they're still human instead of machines."

"I'll be fine, Daddy. I told Mom, I have to learn what they're like if I'm going to help you with your work when I graduate."

"I know, Cassie, but I don't have to like it." James sat down on the bed and checked the old-fashioned analog watch on his wrist. "When did you say your roommate was getting here?"

Cass stammered an answer after an awkward pause. "Uh, she said sometime late this afternoon or this evening. She's traveling in from visiting relatives out of town I think."

"It's such a shame we won't be able to meet Shelby," Faye said. "It would be nice to get to know your new roommate. I'd like to know she's the right kind of person to be sharing a room with you."

"It's fine, Mom. I've talked to her by face chat several times. I promise she's not an ax murderer. She's a really nice girl."

Elena giggled. "Does that mean you two are going to be girl-friends?" Her sister wrapped her arms around her shoulders and made kissing noises.

Cass started to say something but her mother beat her to it.

"Elena, leave your sister alone. She'll find someone new when the time is right." Faye turned to Cass. "I still don't know why you broke up with Susan. She was such a nice girl and you two could have kept things going. Your father and I liked her and she comes from such a good family."

Cass groaned. The last thing she wanted was a discussion with her parents about her love life. "Susan and I parted on good terms, Mom. We both decided we didn't want a long-distance relationship."

"It's only long distance because you didn't choose to go to the same college as Susan," James said. "You could still change your mind, you know. It's not too late. You know enrollment in a Sapiens school is guaranteed to children of members. I had a difficult time explaining to our friends why you didn't choose to go to an approved educational institution."

"If I'm going to be a politician and lawyer like you, Dad, I need to go to a good school with a program that affords me the opportunities you had. I thought you would've understood that by now."

"I do," James said. He glanced towards the closed door again. "I just don't like you being around all these people who aren't like us. Things were different, safer when I went to school. We didn't have the opportunities offered to us now."

"That's why I'm here, Daddy. I need to see how things are in the world if I'm going to help you bring about change for people like us."

Cass resisted the urge to bite her lip. She didn't want her father to see through her lie. While she held some of her parents' technophobic views about body enhancements using cybernetics, she wasn't quite as rabid about it. She believed in most of the Sapiens movement's core values guarding against artificial intelligence's intrusion into the world. Some of their views were a bit too extreme, though.

The Sapiens movement stood against all uses of artificial intelligence, seeing it as the eventual doom of humanity. Because of that, anyone who received any sort of electronic addition to their bodies, whether medically necessary or merely cosmetic, was considered less than fully human anymore. Most add-ons included cybernetic implants connecting to the Mantle.

The Mantle was an overarching artificial intelligence network that offered connectivity to all robots and cybernetic devices. It allowed autonomous robots to operate and navigate in a complex three-dimensional human world. For connected humans, it was an exponential leap beyond the simpler internet of the early twenty-first century.

That was why James and many members of conservative organizations like the Sapiens movement referred to all people with such connected enhancements as "subs," short for sub-human. It was considered a derogatory term by most, but in Sapiens' circles and especially in their sheltered and gated enclaves, it was accepted as normal.

Cass glanced at the watch her father gave her on her twelfth birthday, a battery-operated analog model from a different age. It was later than she thought and things were going to be cut a little too close with Shelby's arrival if she didn't hurry things along.

"Hey, I've got an orientation thing to go to this afternoon. Is it all right if I finish putting away the rest of my things myself? I can unpack the remaining boxes. You all can go ahead and head on home."

"Are you sure?" her mom asked. She crossed the room and put an arm around Cass's shoulders. "We don't mind staying here and finishing up while you go to your thing. Maybe we'll get a chance to meet Shelby, if she gets here before we leave—"

"Um, no, really, that's all right," Cass interrupted her mom. "Like I said, I'm pretty sure Shelby will be here much later. She's coming from quite a distance. You guys should get on the road. You'll all want to get home in good time."

"Cassie's right," her father said. "It's time for our girl to step out on her own, Faye. We need to let her do her own thing."

"Thanks, Dad. Really, I'll make sure to call all of you tonight and tell you about everything I learned at orientation. We can face chat when I get back to my room later or maybe tomorrow if it's too late."

Cass's mom looked disappointed and didn't hide it well. She smiled and gave Cass a big hug. Her father did the same.

Elena came over and hugged her big sister, too. As she leaned in, Elena whispered in her ear. "If you find a hot, new girlfriend, make sure you let me know first."

"Don't worry, Elena. You'll be the first person I tell."

Cass smiled as her mom, sister, and father all turned to leave. She remembered at the last minute to grab her new room key from the desktop. The plastic card was her pass not only to get into the building and her room, it also was used to access the other facilities and buildings on campus. If she forgot it, or lost it, the dorm monitor would charge her account to let her back into the room.

She slid the card into the back pocket of her shorts and pulled the door closed as she followed her parents out into the hallway.

Outside, in front of the dorm, lines of cars waited behind those unloading all the incoming freshmen's luggage and personal items. Seeing the backup, Cass was glad she'd convinced her parents to get here early, for several reasons.

Cass stopped at the curb beside their car. Elena jumped in the back of her dad's official company sedan, already slipping on her headphones and pulling up something on her tablet to watch.

"Goodbye, pumpkin," James said as he hugged her. "I'm proud of you for stepping out like this. Risk-takers are just the kind of people our movement needs right now. When you graduate, the company will be proud to hire you."

James Armstrong's company provided consulting and lobbying support to Sapiens' political candidates around the country.

Cass nodded and smiled at her father's words. "Thanks, Dad. I'll do my best."

She waved as her mom and dad got in the car and drove from the parking lot. Cass followed the car with her eyes until it was out of sight, leaving her alone and on her own for the first time in her life.

She smiled and looked around at her new classmates. Her father was right. It was a bit of a shock to see the few people with cyber enhancements all mixing with normal people like herself. All of the add-ons she saw were voluntary and mostly cosmetic. It had become quite the fashion statement for some people, although they were still very much in the minority, even here on a progressive university campus full of young people.

Cass went back into the dorm and returned to her room to finish unpacking. She thought her parents would never leave. They seemed to be dragging out the whole move-in process on purpose despite her best efforts to hurry them along.

She accomplished the mission of the day, though. She got them on the road home several hours before Shelby's scheduled arrival. That was important. Cass didn't really have an orientation meeting that afternoon. It was scheduled for much later that evening after dinner. The real reason her parents needed to leave had to do with her new roommate, Shelby Moore.

Cass knew from the first time she saw her prospective roommate via a private face chat that her father and mother definitely wouldn't approve of Shelby.

Chapter 2

WHEN THE DORM room door opened less than an hour later, it caught Cass by surprise. She'd been sitting on her bed, listening to high-energy dance music on her headphones when the raven-haired girl bounced into her room. The flicker of movement she saw out of the corner of her eye made Cass jump to her feet.

To say Shelby Moore was the opposite of Cass Armstrong was an understatement. The two of them couldn't be more different. Cass had strawberry blonde hair, long enough to hang down past her shoulders to the small of her back, which was how she preferred to wear it. Shelby's shorter, dark hair reached just to the nape of her neck. While Cass was of average height for a woman, the newcomer was taller by several inches.

The most striking difference, however was the cybernetic extension on her left arm, replacing her entire forearm and hand. She also had several v-tats visible across her neck and right forearm. Each played a series of recorded animations. The images looked like Manga characters. Cass knew from her previous conversations with Shelby there were others playing in more intimate locations on the girl's body.

"Hey, roomie," the newcomer said. "Didn't mean to scare you."

"It's all right," Cass said, taking off her headphones and dropping them on the bed. She glanced at her watch. "I didn't expect you for another few hours."

"I managed to catch an earlier bullet train down from Boston. I wanted to get my things moved in before it got dark. Besides, we have a bunch of cool things going on tonight to kick off our freshman year. I heard they're going to give us a whole lot of free stuff just for showing up."

Cass nodded. She'd heard the same thing from their dorm's upperclass hall monitor. Cass looked out into the hallway behind Shelby. "Do you need help carrying anything in?"

"Yeah, I had the van driver help me unload everything at the curb outside. That's actually why I came in to check and see if you were here. I was hoping you'd be here to help me." Shelby looked around the room. "Did your folks leave already?"

"My parents and sister had to leave early," Cass lied. "I think they had something going on this evening back home."

"I'm sorry I missed them. If I'd known they weren't going to stay later, I would have caught the first train down this morning."

"It's all right, I'm sure you'll get a chance to meet them another time."

As she spoke, Cass caught herself staring at Shelby's left arm. The mechanical fingers looked almost like normal ones, except for the smooth metallic skin. The thought of self-mutilation like that intrigued her in a horrific sort of way. She couldn't think of anything that would make her do something like that.

She yearned to ask Shelby a ton of questions about how the arm felt and if getting it or her v-tats installed was painful. The only thing she knew about such things came from the Sapiens educational programs she'd had in the enclave's school about the practice of what her people called cyber-butchery. Based on what she'd learned, the changes were excruciating and not something any sane person would do willingly.

Shelby caught her staring and held up her left hand. "You like my new arm? I got it done up in Boston while visiting my family a few weeks ago. It was a gift from my older brother, Eric, as a going-away to school present."

Shelby reached over with her right hand and tapped a place on the metal skin of her left forearm. A panel popped open, revealing a hidden compartment. She reached in and pulled out a piece of gum.

Popping it in her mouth, she asked, "Do you want some?" Shelby extended her left arm towards Cass, offering gum from the hidden compartment.

Cass flinched away from the metal appendage before she could stop herself. The reaction was a reflex and she tried, without success, to hide the brief instant of horror she felt at almost touching the cybernetic limb. Cass caught herself with a mental admonishment, "Chill, Cassie. It's not a disease."

She tried masking her initial reaction by waving a hand of dismissal at Shelby. "Uh, no, that's okay. I'm not much of a gum person. That's pretty cool, though."

"Yeah, it is," Shelby replied, seeming not to notice her roommate's reaction. "My brother gave me enough to have them replace my entire arm with a new one. I opted for just the forearm but with some extra add-ons. Look, now I don't need to carry any school supplies with me at all."

Shelby held up her metal hand and raised her index finger. The rounded tip of the finger opened and turned into a stylus. She extended all her fingers. Each of them now displayed a different fixture or tool.

Shelby laughed as she wiggled her fingers. "It's like the ultimate pocket knife, but built into my hand. We shouldn't have a problem with needing any tools around the room. I've got them all covered right here."

Cass tried not to wince again as she heard the faint whine of the mechanical servos in her roommate's arm. A part of her, deep inside, had the morbid desire to reach out and run her fingertips over the lifeless, mechanical forearm. She wondered, was it cold and hard like the outer sheet metal skin of a machine, or warm with the heat of Shelby's body like a living limb.

Cass caught herself staring at it again. When she'd first met

Shelby via face chat, the only enhancements her roommate had were a few v-tats and the cerebral control interface implant beside her left ear. That was already extreme enough in Cass's mind.

This artificial arm was something else entirely. The thought of replacing an entire body part with a cybernetic replacement was beyond alien to Cass. It hadn't occurred to her that Shelby would have gotten another enhancement before they met in person.

Cass wanted to understand why someone would do something like that to themselves. If she was going to join the Sapiens political strategy team alongside her father, she needed to understand the mindset that would allow someone to intentionally destroy their humanity that way.

Cass had learned a lot about Shelby via their conversations over the summer. Those initial chats challenged a lot of her conservative views and stereotypes about cyber-humans like Shelby. Cass now questioned many things she learned while growing up in the enclave.

"Hey," Cass said, changing the subject. "Let's go out and bring your stuff inside before somebody grabs it for themselves."

"Nobody will do that," Shelby said. She reached up and tapped the small metal implant visible just in front of her left ear. "I deployed a remote drone to monitor all my stuff. It's all still there. I can see it right now. Anybody who tries to steal it, will get to hear me yelling at them while I run out there and teach them the error of their ways."

Cass laughed at the expression on Shelby's face. She looked so fierce all of the sudden. Even the scrolling v-tats on her neck and right arm changed to reflect her mood. They shifted to animations of snarling tigers as she voiced her threat. While cyber enhancements seemed alien to Cass, some things were pretty awesome in an ornamental sense.

Once again, Cass found herself wanting to reach out and touch her new roommate's enhancements. What did the skin over a v-tat feel like? She had so many questions for her roommate. Shelby intrigued her.

Cass resisted the urge again, instead lifting her arm to point to the door. "Let's go get your stuff. We have a bunch of activities coming up this evening and I'm kind of hungry. We can get your stuff moved in and then go find some food. I think there's an ice cream social some time this afternoon."

"Ice cream sounds awesome," Shelby said. "You're right, let's get my stuff. There's a sundae out there with my name on it."

The two women headed out of the room to start carrying in the boxes Shelby had piled out at the curb. Despite their different backgrounds, Cass found herself drawn to Shelby's charismatic personality. She seemed so full of energy and excitement, in contrast to Cass's more introverted nature.

It didn't take the two of them long to carry everything back inside. Cass saw a bunch of items similar to hers. There was no evidence of a tablet computer like the one she brought to school, though. She wondered how Shelby planned on accessing their assignments and class reading.

Once the two of them were back in the room and unpacking Shelby's things, Cass asked about her roommate's lack of a physical computer.

"You still use a tablet?" Shelby asked in reply. She laughed and gestured to her head. "I got the full integrated educational implant upgrade last year. I'm tied directly into the Mantle now."

Cass gasped, "Aren't you afraid the AI will take you over in your sleep?"

Shelby's puzzled frown caught her by surprise.

Cass realized she'd reacted poorly and covered her exclamation by adding, "I always figured the Mantle's cyber brain would be so alien to us it would confuse a person who was tied in directly to it."

Cass grew up hearing stories of rogue vigilante robots attacking people and about the Mantle randomly frying people's brains after the connection was made.

Shelby laughed and shook her head. "Not at all. It's really liberating. Because the campus systems are connected to the Mantle's interface, too, I'm tied in to everything that happens here. I don't have to take notes in class or anything like that. I can access the original lecture recording, with video and audio, anytime I want.

Not only that, but I have access to the direct text transcripts so the lectures are searchable. It makes research and homework super easy."

"Isn't that cheating? What about when you take a test?"

"Oh, the professor can turn off access locally. The classrooms utilize a sort of virtual Faraday cage to shut down my implant's access during tests and quizzes. That ensures I actually learn the material." Shelby turned and stared at Cass. "You have a lot of questions. How is it you don't know this stuff?"

"My tablet isn't connected to the Mantle, just to basic services and public databases."

"It's not? How do you search for anything? How do you live?"

Shelby's question irked Cass. She'd been avoiding the topic of her family's aversion to anything in the form of advanced AI-connected technologies. This was a topic she had stayed away from during all their private chats over the summer. Cass was afraid of what Shelby would think. She didn't want to have to explain herself or defend her beliefs and the way she'd been raised.

Cass shrugged and tried to blow it off. "My family just doesn't like a lot of the new technologies out there today, that's all."

"What do you mean? You aren't like those crazy people in the Sapiens movement, are you?"

When Cass didn't answer the question right away and looked away instead, Shelby barked out an awkward laugh. "Oh, my God, your family are Sapiens members? I can't believe you didn't tell me."

Shelby raised her arm, noticing Cass's involuntary flinch this time. "I suppose you think it's fun to have some kind of freak as your roommate? Are you going to brag to all your Sapiens high school friends about your pet subhuman?"

Cass shook her head. This was going all wrong. "No, it's not like that. I wanted to meet new people and learn about people like you."

"People like me? I'm not any different than you just because I have this arm or any other enhancement. I'm as human as you are."

"That's not what I meant, Shelby—"

"I thought all you Sapiens members hated people like me?

That's why you live behind the walls of your private enclaves, isn't it?"

"We don't hate you, we just don't want to be like you," Cass blurted out, trying to get a word in around Shelby's shouting. "All we want is to remain human."

Shelby put her hands on her hips and cocked her head to one side. The snarling tigers were back on her arm and neck. "So now I'm not human to you? You know, I read the crap you people put out there in your flyers and so-called safety notices about the dangers of cyber-humans like me. I know fear and hatred when I see it. I've heard of the things that people like you do to people like me."

"None of that stuff really happens," Cass said. "You're just repeating fake news. The violence you talk about isn't real. Nobody I know would hurt anyone unless someone attacked them first. We're peaceful. The goal of the Sapiens movement is to protect humanity from the dangers of too much integration between humans and technology."

Shelby scowled at her. The metal hand balled up into a fist to match the other one, just as a real hand would. It was as if it really was a part of her body. Cass knew it wasn't, of course. It was a metal construct, something that had been added by medical doctors who were better described as butchers than healers.

Shelby caught Cass staring at her cybernetic forearm. She lifted it and held it right in front of her roommate's face.

Cass flinched backwards again and raised her hands up to block what she thought was an incoming attack. "So now you're going to hit me? I'm just telling you how I feel, how I was raised."

Shelby snorted and lowered her arm. "I wouldn't hit you. I wouldn't waste the energy. I just figured you'd want to get a close-up look at my defect, my deformity." She lifted her arm again. "Go ahead. Take a look. Don't you want to touch it? It's just as much a part of me as my other hand."

"No, it's not," Cass shot back. "You had your real hand chopped off so you could have that thing put on your arm."

"That thing, as you put it, is part of me. I can sense and feel through it. I can pick things up. I can touch you and feel the goose bumps I see raised on your arm. It's as much a part of me is anything else on my body."

This whole argument was a disaster. Nothing was going the way Cass had expected. She'd been fascinated with Shelby's magnetic personality and her enhancements since their first face chat. Cass merely wanted to understand why anyone would do such a thing to themselves. But her questions now all seemed wrong and invasive. Shelby actually believed the horrible things she said about Cass and her family just because they rightly feared the takeover by AI in the world. She had to find a way to salvage this.

"Shelby, I don't want to fight with you. We just met in person for the first time. I didn't have time to tell you about my family. We only talked a few times before and they were just short face chats. I didn't intentionally hide anything from you."

"But you did. I should've known something was off about you as soon as I did a routine search for you and came up with nothing. You know there's absolutely no record of you beyond your initial birth record in the system at all."

"Of course. That's the point. There's no reason for humans to be so connected to everything. My family scrubs all mention of us from the system. It's to protect me and my sister. Keeping us off the AI databases is one way to do that."

"So, I suppose you live in one of those weird Sapiens communities where no AI is allowed inside the gates? Would I even be allowed to enter if I showed up?"

Cass wasn't sure what to say. Shelby obviously knew enough about the movement and the private enclaves to know the answer to that question. She knew all about how the Armstrong family, and others like them, separated themselves from the rest of society to protect their families from the inevitable.

"You don't understand why we live apart. It's not about being welcome, Shelby. It's about protecting ourselves. You've put far too much trust in what technology can offer you without understanding the risks involved. I learned to understand those risks and be wary of them."

"So, I suppose your family are friends with people like Sterling Noble and his goons. That asshole wants to make people like me against the law. He wants to make us all second-class citizens."

"Mr. Noble is not like that. He wants to protect the people who don't choose to integrate themselves with technology. That's all. It shouldn't be something that holds us back just because we don't want to be as connected or dependent on technology the way you are."

"Mr. Noble? You mean you've met him?"

"He's been over for dinner a few times. My father is one of his political consultants on technology risks."

Shelby spun around and stalked away across the room, her hands in the air. She stopped and looked out the window. Shelby shook her head. "So, my roommate is not only a Sapiens member, she's also a personal friend of that racist bigot Sterling Noble, too."

Shelby turned to face Cass and rolled her eyes. "How the hell did I get myself into this mess."

Cass held out her hand. "Shelby, I don't want to be enemies. I came to a school outside our closed educational system so that I could learn more about everyone else in the world. I realize I was raised separate and sheltered. I came here to understand why you did what you did to yourself and why your parents let you do it." Cass barely stopped herself from using the word "mutilate."

"My parents were wise enough to let me be me, Cass. They made me hold off until I was sixteen, but that's just the law. My mom and dad didn't fill my head full of hatred and lies."

Cass started to shout a response in defense of her family but stopped when there was a knock at the door. Both she and Shelby stopped and glanced at the closed door to the room. Neither made a move to open it.

After a few seconds, the person knocked again, "Ladies, open the door. It's Mitch, your dorm monitor. Everyone on the floor can hear you two yelling at each other."

Shelby moved to the door before Cass could recover from the shock and embarrassment at Mitch's words.

As she pulled the door open, Shelby said, "I'm glad you're here. I want a new roommate. I can't live with her."

Mitch, a senior who made extra money working for the school as a dorm monitor, sighed. "Why do you want a new roommate?"

His bored tone and attitude angered Cass. It was like he didn't take Shelby seriously. She didn't want to change roommates but this guy didn't seem to care one way or the other and that infuriated her.

"She's a Sapiens racist. She called me a sub freak."

"I did not."

"You may as well have. I can't even think about staying in the same room with you tonight." Shelby turned back to Mitch. "Put me in another room."

"There are no other rooms. This dorm is full. Everyone else already has a roommate."

"What about other dorms? There's got to be a room somewhere?" Shelby sounded almost desperate.

"Look, there will be an opportunity to change rooms and swap with someone else in a few weeks, once things settle down. Until then, you two will just have to get along."

Cass stepped forward. She was worried now about how Shelby might react to being forced to stay. Was she safe in the room with her now that Shelby hated her?

"I'm not sure we can do that," Cass said. "I'm not the person she says I am but now I'm afraid she might attack me or something."

"What? So now I'm some sort of animal who can't control myself?"

Mitch put up his hands. "Ladies, ladies. There's literally nothing I can do to change your room assignments. What I can do is write you both up with causing a disturbance in the dorm."

That stopped both Shelby and Cass in their tracks. Cass had never been in trouble in her life and now she was going to be sent to the Dean or something like that.

A glance at Shelby revealed she might be having similar thoughts.

Taking advantage of the silence, Mitch continued. "I don't have to do that, though, if you two will do what I say."

"What's that?" Shelby asked.

"I want you both to leave the room and go, together, to the ice cream social over at the student center. Get some food there and sit down in public for a while. Maybe out in the open, the two of you can work out your differences without shouting hateful things at each other. Deal?"

"And if we don't?" Cass asked.

"Then you can visit the Dean, together for fighting and causing a disturbance in the dorm. You'll still end up staying together but you'll have the added benefit of getting some joint community service hours around campus on top of it."

Cass stole a glance in Shelby's direction. Shelby returned it then said, "Fine, I'll go, but you can't make me talk to her."

"No, I can't, but here are the rules. You two have to go together, sit together while you eat, and return together. Otherwise, I'll start the report now and send you to the Dean."

"You don't have to do that," Cass blurted out. "We'll do it, right Shelby? Just don't write us up."

Shelby nodded after a brief pause and Cass sighed. She was afraid Shelby was too upset to see reason.

"Excellent," Mitch said. His pleasant grin irked Cass. "Grab your keys and go. I don't want to see either of you back here for at least an hour."

Cass walked over to her desk and grabbed her key card. Shelby waited for her by the door.

Cass stalked past her and headed down the hallway, her mind spinning with ways to fix the horrible mess she'd made getting to know Shelby.

Chapter 3

THE TWO GIRLS walked in silence across the campus to the student center. It held the cafeteria, school bookstore and gift shop, as well as the activities center, weight room, and indoor track.

There was a long line leading up to the table where they dipped the ice cream. Cass tried to fill the silence by scanning the fixings table where people could add toppings and flavored syrups to their choice of ice cream.

She started putting together her options and choices in her mind as they passed by in line. Before she knew it, she turned to Shelby and said, "I'm getting crushed chocolate cookies and caramel syrup on mine."

"Hmph," Shelby said in reply. She crossed her arms and stared straight ahead.

"Seriously," Cass said. "What's wrong with what I just said?"

Shelby didn't say anything at first. When Cass stood and stared at her, waiting for a reply, Shelby finally broke down and answered.

"Caramel and chocolate? First of all, pick one or the other. They don't mix. Second, you missed the best part of the toppings."

"What's that?" Cass asked, glancing at the table again.

"The gummy bears. They are the obvious choice when they're available."

"Ewww. I like gummy bears, but not on my ice cream. They get all hard and chewy in the cold, and get stuck in your teeth."

"That's the best part." Shelby smiled. "You save some for later."

"Gross."

Cass's response made Shelby laugh out loud.

It caught Cass by surprise and before she knew it, she laughed, too. "We can't even get along about our ice cream options. That's pretty sad."

"So much for Mitch's grand plan to get us to agree on something."

"I know, right?" Cass said. "He acted like he was bored by our fight, like we were interrupting something he had to do."

"Yeah, if he acts like that all the time, it's going to be awful having him living on the floor with us the whole year." Shelby glanced at Cass. "I guess that's one thing we agree on, at least."

Cass nodded. She realized Shelby had offered a cease fire to their argument with that last statement. It was her turn.

"Shelby, I'm sorry about what I said. I'm trying to learn all these new things and sometimes I say stuff without realizing it."

"I just wish you'd told me about your family over the summer."

"Would you have agreed to room with me if I had?" Cass asked.

Shelby didn't answer.

"I didn't think so," Cass said. "Look, I want to learn more about the things they taught me growing up. I know now so much of what I learned isn't like they told me it would be out here in the rest of the world."

"I can't even understand what it was like growing up there like that. Did you have any access to the net or anything?"

Cass shrugged. "We had a closed network inside the community. That gave filtered access to outside information and news feeds. It was enough to do school projects and stuff like that."

"What about VR gaming?"

"Oh, no, nothing like that. That's giving yourself over to influence from the AI. The name says it all. Virtual reality isn't actual reality. How are you supposed to tell what's fake from real if you do that too much?"

"Weird. I can't even think what it would be like without any sort of VR gaming. I'd be so bored all the time. What did you do?"

"I read books. I like stories about kids like me growing up in the past."

The line had moved forward far enough that Cass and Shelby were next. Cass grabbed a bowl and handed it to Shelby before grabbing another for herself.

"We've got chocolate, vanilla, and strawberry," the girl behind the table said.

"I'll take two scoops of vanilla," Cass said. She handed the other girl her bowl and waited while another older student dipped the ice cream for her.

When she got her bowl back, she moved on to the toppings table. Shelby was right behind her. She'd gotten two dips of chocolate.

They both laughed as Shelby went right for the gummy bears, spooning so many atop her ice cream that a few fell off the sides to the floor.

Cass bent down and helped pick them up and throw them in the trash before finishing making her own sundae. She put crushed cookie topping on hers and then caramel as promised. She topped it all off with whipped cream from an aerosol can at the end of the table.

"Want some?" Cass offered Shelby the whipped cream.

"Sure," Shelby said, holding out her bowl.

Cass squirted a generous pile of whipped cream on top of the gummy bear laden bowl. Shelby nodded and grabbed a spoon for each of them as they moved away from the line.

"Let's sit over here," Shelby said, pointing to a bench in front of the bookstore entrance.

Cass followed her over and sat down next to Shelby. For the next minute or so, the two of them enjoyed their ice cream in silence.

Cass was the first to speak up again. "So, can we stand to live together until they approve a change of room?"

"We don't have to change rooms, Cass, at least not right now. You shouldn't have hidden who you were from me, though."

When Cass started to respond, Shelby held up a hand to stop her. "I understand why you did it. I just wish you didn't feel like you had to hide who you were from me."

"I'm still the same me you talked to all summer, the only difference is now you know where I grew up. I'm not defined by that, Shelby. I don't believe everything I learned back in the enclave schools."

Shelby turned to face Cass on the bench. "What have you learned is different?"

"I've learned that just because you have add-ons and enhancements, it doesn't mean you're under control of the Mantle. You're just like me in most ways, the ways that really matter."

"And, what have you learned is the same as you heard growing up?"

That question was hard for Cass to answer. She didn't know where to start because she was still learning so much about the world outside the enclave.

"I honestly don't know yet. I guess that list is a work in progress."

Shelby smiled. "Good answer."

"It's the truth."

"I know, Cass. That's why it's a good answer. Look, I made some snap judgements about you earlier, too. I have to hold myself accountable if I'm going to take you to task."

They finished the last of their ice cream and stood to throw the bowls away. Together, they turned back towards the dorm.

Cass had a random thought and laughed out loud.

"What?" Shelby asked.

"Oh, I was thinking about how smug Mitch is going to be if we come back and we're no longer fighting."

"The hell with Mitch. I gave up worrying about what boys think about me a long time ago. It's much more important to me what you think."

They walked a bit longer then Shelby smiled.

Cass glanced her way and asked, "What are you smiling at?"

"I know how to get Mitch. Let's make him think his plan worked too well."

"What?"

"We're almost there. Hold my hand."

Cass looked down. Shelby held out her cybernetic hand to her. Cass swallowed hard and reached down, taking the metal hand in her own.

She was struck immediately by how warm it was to the touch. The smooth metal wasn't cold at all. It wasn't soft like skin, but it still felt alive somehow. That surprised her. She stroked the back of the hand with her thumb.

"Stop that. It tickles," Shelby said.

"You can feel that?"

"Of course, I can. What good would it be if I couldn't feel something touching my hand? The neural-mechanical connections allow for all the basic senses: hot, cold, pressure. It can even generate a diminished pain response if the arm is damaged in some way."

"Wow, I had no idea."

"Let's set some ground rules from here on out," Shelby suggested. "If you have a question about my arm or my v-tats or anything else, just ask. Don't assume you understand. I will do the same about your parents, family and friends growing up."

"That sounds good," Cass replied.

"Awesome. Now, ready to go inside and blow Mitch's mind?"

Cass nodded and with a burst of laughter, the two roommates entered the dorm and headed back to their room.

Chapter 4

THE VISIT to the ice cream social on the first day on campus started to cement the friendship between the two roommates. Cass was glad. There was a lot to like about Shelby, despite her implants.

The two of them came up with some additional rules to help them avoid sensitive topics unless they had to time to sit down and make sure there were no misunderstandings regarding technology and enhancements. Instead, the two girls focused on their past activities in high school and what it was like growing up in their families.

They both had broken up with long-time girlfriends over the summer. They talked a lot about how hard it was to leave all their friends behind. Those discussions helped to draw them closer over the following weeks as school got underway and the stress of studying began.

Shelby talked about her older brother most. He'd already graduated from the same university they attended and now worked as a social worker in the city nearby. His job involved working with transient and homeless communities around the area.

Shelby's animated tone when talking about him showed her pride in him. It made Cass want to meet him someday and she asked Shelby when he would be on campus.

For some reason, Shelby hesitated answering Cass about her brother coming to visit.

"He's really busy, Cass. I don't think he has a lot of time to drop everything he's doing all the time and come here to visit me."

"Even on the weekends?"

"Yeah, especially then." Shelby looked away as she answered.

"Shel, what aren't you telling me? Remember we agreed not to hide things from each other. Our rules still apply."

"Eric is a bit of an activist for the cyber-human community."

"Okay, so?" Cass asked.

"I haven't told him about your family and where you come from. He's super-focused right now on the Sapiens movement."

Cass paused. She'd never mentioned that before.

"Focused how?"

"Well, he's convinced he's uncovered evidence of a Sapiens First cell in the city."

Cass laughed. "Sapiens First is a myth perpetrated by people opposed to the movement. There is no secret terrorist arm of the Sapiens Movement."

"And that's why I haven't invited Eric to come meet you. I don't want the two of you getting into an argument."

"I wouldn't start a fight with him. He's your brother, Shelby."

"For now, the two of you should hold off on meeting each other, alright?"

Cass nodded and let it drop. It wasn't worth arguing about. Shelby was the only friend Cass had at school. She missed all her friends from high school. Most of them enrolled at the nearest Sapiens higher education program and she'd seen some messages from a few of them that indicated they were having a great time away at school.

For Cass, that wasn't the case. She had worked things out with Shelby and the two of them grew closer as the weeks passed by.

Shelby always asked Cass to accompany her when she went out to do things with other friends from school. Cass refused, citing her schoolwork or the need to call her parents. Shelby surprised her on more than one occasion when she opted to cancel her plans and hang out in the room with her, sharing funny stories about the various people she knew around campus. Cass came to relish the times her roommate stuck around to spend with her.

Other than Shelby, though, Cass found it hard to make friends with the other students around her. She feared they'd hold her Sapiens background against her, so she avoided sharing any details about herself. That caused others to pull away from her and gravitate towards those who were more outgoing. It wasn't that they didn't like her, it was worse. They stopped noticing her altogether.

Cass got over the lack of a social life by staying focused on her studies instead, as her attempts to make friends didn't pan out. As she dug into her own school work more and more, Cass noticed right away how Shelby didn't seem to spend as much time on it as she did. She studied in a different way than Cass did.

It took Cass a while to realize it had to do with her cerebral implant that made the difference. While Cass poured over the carefully typed notes in her tablet, Shelby would lean back in the chair at her desk or on her bed and close her eyes.

At first, Cass thought her roommate was sleeping all the time. Shelby laughed when Cass asked her about the constant napping.

"Do you have to sleep a lot more because of the implant? You're always napping while I'm here studying."

"No, silly, I'm studying just like you. My implant connects to the university's auto recordings of all the class lectures. They're indexed and transcribed so I can jump right to the parts I need to review without having to listen to the whole thing. It's super-efficient."

Cass wondered what it must be like to be able to review things that way. As she pondered it, though, the thought sent a shiver down her spine. Studying that way let the machines and AI into Shelby's head. It scared Cass to even think about being connected and exposed to the whole world via the Mantle that way.

Shelby's study regimen was so different and took so much less time, she spent much more time out socializing than Cass did. Over the next few weeks, Cass became more and more isolated and lonely.

The only break came when she went home for the weekend for

Elena's birthday. It only served to compound her loneliness. Her mother talked the whole time about all the updates she got from the other enclave mothers about Cass's friends who were all away at college together.

She returned to school from that weekend even more depressed. Shelby wasn't there and Cass didn't even bother to turn the lights on when she came in the room. She dropped her backpack on the floor and flopped down on the bed, staring at the ceiling while she lay there in the dark.

Shelby returned, bubbling with energy as usual, entering the room and flicking the lights on while chatting over her implant's comm interface with one of her friends. "…Yeah, I just need to grab a sweater. It's going to be chilly tonight. I'll be right there and we can leave." She paused for a few seconds and then said, "Great! See you soon."

She turned and spotted Cass on the bed. "Oh, sorry, Cassie. I didn't know you were back already. Were you sleeping?"

"No, not really. Just thinking."

"In a dark room? Did everything go all right on your trip home? You were at your sister's birthday, right?

"Yes, it was fine," she said as she sat up. "Elena got some nice stuff."

"Well, something is wrong." Shelby sat on the end of Cass's bed. She reached out with one hand and placed it on her roommate's shoulder. "What happened that put you in a funk?"

"I guess it was my mother. She kept going on about all my old high school friends and how much fun they're having at school. Most of them went off to the same place together. After hearing her go on about all the things she's heard about them from their parents, I feel so disconnected to everything that used to be big parts of my life."

Shelby smiled and nodded as she listened to Cass share what was bothering her. Cass noticed right away how much better she felt just talking to Shelby about it. She was always a good listener.

"I'm sorry, Shel. I feel like I'm always dropping my sad, depressing problems on you."

"I don't mind. I tell you when stuff is wrong, too. We're here for each other. That's what friends are for."

Cass didn't say anything. She shrugged and stared at the floor by her bed.

"You know what?" Shelby said. "We need to get you out of here. Let's go grab something at the Special Grind cafe off campus. It'll be good to get out in public around people for a while."

"I thought you had plans already tonight. I heard you talking about it when you came in."

"That? Oh, that was nothing major. I'll tell them you got home early and we are heading out to grab something to eat together. They'll understand. It's just Lisa and a few other people from one of my classes."

"You talk about Lisa a lot. Is she cute?"

"Yeah, you might say that. It doesn't matter, though, because I'm here with you, now."

Shelby stood up and grabbed Cass's coat from the floor by her back pack. She tossed the coat on the bed. "Come on. We'll have fun. We can try and guess what weird jobs people have as they come in to the cafe. That's always fun."

Cass smiled. They'd played that game before. It always ended up with the two of them giggling in hysterics as they each tried to come up with the more outrageous profession. She stood up and put on her coat.

"Good," Shelby said. "You feel better already, don't you?"

"Yeah," Cass admitted. "It's annoying how good you are at that."

"At what?"

"Making me feel better. How come you're so good at that?"

"I am a psych major. It's what I want to do. I've always been good at helping people around me. My mother says it's my calling."

"I think she's right," Cass said as she headed to the door behind Shelby. "Hey, Shel."

Shelby stopped and turned to look her way. "Yeah?"

"Thanks."

Shelby's infectious grin spread across her face. "Sure thing, Roomie. We've got to stick up for each other, don't we?"

Cass smiled back and nodded then followed Shelby out and down the hallway. Cass's connection to her roommate seemed to grow each time the two of them went out together like this. She liked it and wondered if it meant there was more there than just a friendship between two roommates.

<hr>

Chapter 5

<hr>

A FEW WEEKS LATER, right before fall break, Shelby bounced into their room right after lunch one day, humming to herself.

Cass looked up from studying for her intro to poly-sci midterm. The approaching exams frightened her a little and she wanted to be prepared for anything the professors might throw her way. She scowled at Shelby as the girl puttered around the room humming to herself. The noise her roommate made irked Cass. Shelby was singing along with a song playing in her head via her Mantle connection.

"Hey, can you keep it down? I'm studying for my poly-sci test."

"Oh, sorry. I'm kind of excited. I got an awesome invite today."

"What's it for?" Cass asked.

"Remember Lisa, from my psychology class? She asked me if I wanted to go with her and some of her other friends to her parents' condo in the Caribbean on our fall break next weekend. We have Friday and Monday off, which would give us plenty of time to hang out on the beach and hit the clubs at night. The plan is to come back late Monday night in time for class Tuesday morning."

"Is this the girl you think is so cute?" Cass asked.

"It is," Shelby said, blushing a little. "But she's got a girlfriend already so I'm outta luck."

The v-tat on the inside of Shelby's right arm changed to a blushing emoji face. It fascinated Cass how the v-tats changed spontaneously when Shelby wasn't paying attention to them.

Cass smiled at her roommate. "That sounds like a lot of fun, Shelby. You should go."

Shelby turned around to look at Cass. "I will if you will."

Cass looked up. The offer caught her by surprise. "Me? I thought maybe you'd want to go by yourself to be with your friends."

"You're my friend too, Cass. You can't stay in our room all the time. Come on. Come with us and have some fun for a change. You're always studying and I don't see you going out with anybody to do anything at all on the weekends."

"Yeah, well I did have to go home that one time for my sister's birthday. The rest of the time, I just felt more like hanging out in the room. Besides, my parents are expecting me home for break."

"Well, I think you should tell your family your plans have changed and you're going to go on this trip with me. You need to get out for a change. Come on, what part of this idea don't you like? Is it the white sandy beaches or the clear, blue water? Just think how much fun it will be to just hang out and do nothing for a change."

Cass did like the beach. The offer tempted her, but she was unsure what her parents would say.

"I'll have to see what my mom and dad say. I'm sure the answer is going to be no."

"Then you have nothing to lose. Let's make a deal. Call them up. If they say no, you don't have to go. But if they say yes, you're in."

Cass was sure her parents would say no to the trip, so the decision to call Shelby's bluff was easy. Shelby didn't understand the dynamic with her parents and how things worked in the Armstrong family. Her parents had always been so protective, there was no way her dad would say yes. He made all the important decisions in the family, and her mother just sort of went along with whatever he wanted.

"I'll have to see what they say. I'm supposed to face chat with them this afternoon. I guess I can bring it up to them. They're not going to say yes, though, so don't count on winning the bet."

"There's no hurry. You can let us know as late as the night before we leave. I'm sure there'll be room on the flight."

Cass smiled as she thought about the offer of the trip. Despite her reservations, the trip sounded fun. Cass knew she'd cut herself off to put some distance between herself and everyone else here on campus. Other than Shelby, Cass avoided talking with anyone unless it was absolutely necessary.

Part of the problem was she didn't want anyone knowing about her family or her father and his position in the Sapiens movement. Her argument with Shelby the first day on campus made her wary of sharing too many details about herself with anyone else. Most other students seemed pretty liberal in their views and the Sapiens movement wasn't popular with most people on campus.

Later that afternoon, while Shelby was at her late class, Cass sat on her bed on face chat with her mother. After a little random conversation, Cass decided to get the request out of the way so when her mother said no, she could move on to talk about when her dad would arrive to pick her up and bring her home for break the next weekend.

"So, Mom, I was wondering if I could go on a weekend outing with Shelby and some of her friends over fall break? We're off from Friday through Monday and they wanted to do something fun together that weekend."

Her mother's response caught Cass completely by surprise.

"Oh, really? That's so funny. Your father and I were just talking about this. You didn't seem to be doing much socializing with anyone there at school and we were both worried you weren't making friends. You should go. If you have something fun to do with friends, that's a better idea than coming home. Where are they planning to go?"

Even though her mom said yes to the initial request, there was no way she'd agree to the actual trip once she had the details. Cass would be leaving the country alone for the first time. Her passport was up-to-date from a family trip to Europe that previous summer so her father could attend a Sapiens Europe event. She'd never gone anywhere on her own before.

Cass stammered a bit as she continued with the trip details. "Uh, there's this resort in the Bahamas they're going to. One of Shelby's friends has a family condo down there."

"All the way to the Bahamas?" Faye asked. "Hmm, I'll have to ask your father. You know how he feels about some of the other countries around the world."

"How I feel about what?" Cass's father asked from off-screen. He must've just walked into the room.

James Armstrong slid into a chair next to Cass's mother and smiled when he spotted his daughter on the screen.

"Hi, Cassie. What's up?" He looked at his wife.

"Cassie wants to go on a trip to the Bahamas with some school friends."

"Yeah, Dad, Shelby invited me to go with her and some other girls from our classes."

Her father glanced at her mother who gave a little shrug. James looked back at Cass and a broad smile crossed his face. "You know what? I think that is a great idea. I've been worried. It seemed like you were always in your room whenever we called. You never talk about anyone but Shelby. It makes me happy you're finally making friends."

"I am not a hermit, Dad. I have made a few friends," Cass lied. "I'm focused on school to make sure I do well in my studies. I want to make you and Mom proud."

"You'll always make us proud," her father said. "There's nothing you can do that won't make us happy. Just be careful. Let me know how much the trip will cost. I'll transfer the money to your account so you can take care of the arrangements. You have your passport with you, right?"

Cass nodded. The shock they'd said yes still kept her from

answering right away. She found her voice after a few seconds. "Yes, yes I do. Um, I don't know what to say."

"You can say thank you," her father replied with a wink.

"Um, sure. Thanks."

"That reminds me," her dad said. "When are we going to get a chance to meet Shelby. Every time we call over there, you tell us she's out of the room."

"Yeah, she's a little bit different from me in that respect. She likes to be out socializing a lot more than I do."

Cass's mother frowned. "She's not partying too much and keeping you from getting things done, is she?"

"No, Mom, she's not like that. She's just out hanging with other friends all the time. She does study in her own way, probably as much as I do."

Cass hoped that answer would put her parents off on the subject of meeting Shelby for a little while. This wasn't the first time they'd pressed her about meeting her roommate.

She knew how they'd react if they saw how many cyber enhancements Shelby had. Cass knew she couldn't keep it a secret from them forever. She also knew her parents were going to freak out when they found out she was living with a cyber-human.

"Maybe, when we come to see you, Shelby can come along and go out to dinner with us?" James offered.

"We'll see, Dad. As I said, she's usually out with friends or watching some event on campus. She's not usually around to do things like that."

"Like what? Hang out with your stuffy parents?" her father asked with a chuckle. "Don't worry about it, Cass. We won't embarrass you in front of her. I promise."

Cass smiled. Her father got along with all of her friends back home. Half of them called him Dad because they were always hanging out at Cass's house. Maybe she was wrong. Maybe he'd get along just as easily with Shelby, too.

"I'll let her know there's a standing offer."

"All right, honey," her mom said. "We've got a dinner tonight with some of our friends from the movement. Sterling is in town and he wants to meet with your dad about an upcoming event."

Her dad smiled and picked up the conversation. "It's actually down there near the university. It would be a great opportunity to show you off to the movement's leadership. There's no time like the present to talk to them about your aspirations to work alongside me when you graduate.

"That would be nice," Cass said. She hesitated a little. Something about having a Sapiens rally so close to campus bothered her.

"Good, I'll let you know my plans when you get back from your trip," James said. "Send me the travel details when you have them along with the cost. I'll forward you the money so you can pay on your end."

"I will. Bye."

"Bye," her parents said as they reached out and closed the connection.

Cass smiled and leaned back in bed and stared at the ceiling. Her parent's unexpected reaction meant Shelby won the bet. She'd be happy Cass would be joining the others on the trip.

Cass pushed down her apprehension and decided it would be nice to do something social and relaxing for a change. She'd never worked as hard as she had these last six weeks. It would be great to not worry about school for a few days.

"You know," Shelby said from the doorway, "You can't keep me a secret from your parents forever."

Cass spun around. "How long have you been standing there?"

"Long enough to realize you still haven't told them about your roommate, the dirty sub."

"Shelby, you know I don't feel that way about you. I'm not ashamed of you or how close we've become. It's just..."

"It's just that you're ashamed of all the things I've done to make me who I am." Shelby held up her enhanced left arm and wiggled her fingers in the air. "You've come to grips with understanding I'm as much a human as you are. Tell them you've had a change of heart and understand things differently now that you've come to know me."

Cass shook her head. "You don't understand. This isn't just something my parents came up with on the fly. My dad and mom are true believers. They think all enhancements, even medical ones, are bad for humanity."

"I get it. They think I'm subhuman since I have non-human parts."

"Don't use that word. I don't call you that."

"Yeah, but you've heard your dad and mom use it before, haven't you? They don't think it's a dirty word. They just use it all the time to describe people like me, don't they?"

Cass frowned but didn't say anything. She couldn't argue with Shelby's insight and she wouldn't lie to her. Shelby knew exactly how her parents talked. She'd probably had people use that word right to her face. Denying her parents talked that way wouldn't change anything.

"Let's change the subject," Cass said. "You and I aren't going to change my parents or their opinions on people with enhancements. At the end of the day, Shel, does it matter what anyone in my family thinks but me?"

"No," Shelby said. To Cass's surprise, she ran her fingers through Cass's hair and brushed a strand away from her face. "It was good news that they're letting you come on the trip with us. It was already going to be fun. It'll be much more so now that I know you're coming along. I'm looking forward to having some quality time alone together."

Cass smiled. "I guess I'm looking forward to it, too. I can't believe my mom and dad actually said yes."

"Me either, honestly. I'm glad they did, though. I'll get you the information on the trip and how you book your flight."

On impulse, Cass reached out and brushed her hand against the back of Shelby's cybernetic hand. She marveled again at the warmth of the metallic appendage. It didn't feel like a machine at all.

"That's only the second time you've touched my arm since we met, Cass. Are you surprised by how real if feels?"

Cass nodded. Her breathing grew faster and could feel her heartbeat through her chest.

"I'm not ashamed of who you are, Shelby. I'm worried how my parents will react, that's all."

"I can take care of myself, Cass. I'm a big girl and I've dealt with people like your father before."

"Not like my father, you haven't. Sometimes I think he would do anything for the movement. He's made comments about some things he and Sterling Noble have discussed. I don't think he knows that I picked up on what he was saying. I'm afraid of what he would do if he found out about you."

Shelby leaned in and tilted Cass's chin up as she bent over. Her lips brushed against Cass's in a gentle caress.

"What about Lisa?" Cass whispered.

"She's not the one I want to go on a trip with. You are, silly."

Cass discovered her own feelings shifting as she finally saw herself through Shelby's eyes. It had never occurred to Cass her roommate would ever be interested in someone like her. As Shelby bent down to kiss her again, Cass realized she was wrong.

Chapter 6

CASS MARVELED at how their relationship changed overnight after that first kiss as she and Shelby planned their trip. Cass's father transferred the money into her account the next day and she booked her flight the day after that.

She got lucky and booked a seat on the same flight with Shelby and the other girls. She even scored the seat next to Shelby.

Cass admitted to herself this get away was sorely needed. After being so focused on her studies and hiding herself away in the dorm room most of the time, the prospect of a Caribbean vacation filled her with a level of anticipation she hadn't felt in a long time. She couldn't wait to get down there and have some time away. It would be an opportunity to explore a new side of her relationship with Shelby.

Cass wasn't new to air travel. She'd flown on family trips a few times before, always on chartered flights with other members of the enclave, though. For her, they'd been fun and full of activities for the children and families in general.

Those chartered jets had been configured for the Sapiens movement passengers so there was no connectivity or AI interface. This was Cass's first trip on a fully connected modern jet, though. When she got on the plane, she marveled at all of the technology advancements this plane had compared to the ones she'd traveled on before.

The seat back in front of her housed a fully automated holographic entertainment center. Its three-dimensional display allowed for full connectivity to the net and Mantle.

After they got settled in their seats before the plane took off, Shelby showed how she connected directly to the plane's entertainment system via her cerebral implant. As Cass watched, Shelby accessed the menus on the holoscreen without having to manually change anything using the touch interface.

The more she thought about the way the airliner's systems connected to the Mantle, the more the whole thing had Cass a little freaked out. She wondered what there was to keep someone from hacking into the plane's flight software and crashing the jet simply to prove a point?

Cass noticed her anxiety level ramping up. She shook her head, trying to put the thoughts of crashing planes out of her mind. The horror stories about the dangers of being connected to the Mantle she'd grown up with, battled with her shifted perspective since she'd been at school. Her point of view had changed a lot since the beginning of the semester, but all the things she'd learned before going away to college weren't erased overnight.

The other four girls traveling with them consisted of two other couples. After meeting them for the first time on the way to the airport that morning, Cass realized Shelby must have planned on making this trip an extended date with Cass the whole time. Lisa had been in a relationship with her girlfriend, Katie, since the beginning of the semester.

Once Cass got over learning about Shelby's secret plan, she settled in to enjoy the trip. She got to know the other two couples and found them fun and likable. This was her first trip with other lesbian couples.

While the Sapiens movement accepted homosexual unions as a matter of course in a modern society, there weren't that many of them. She'd had few role models on which to shape herself and her relationships in middle and high school. As such, she'd kept public displays of affection during her first serious high school relationship with Susan to a minimum when others were around. Now, in the company of other female couples like herself, she enjoyed the new relationship with Shelby even more.

The flight took off without incident and the plane landed in the Bahamas in the late afternoon. After they collected their bags, Shelby connected into the local network and found a ride for the six of them to their resort.

While they waited for the van to arrive, Shelby said, "Cass, I'm accessing the local map and the resort activity schedule now. You won't believe all the stuff that we can do at this place. They have all sorts of excursions and activities we can sign up for. There are horseback riding jaunts down the beach each day and ATV trails through the central part of the island. There are even things like kayak and jet ski rentals that we can take out directly from the beach in front of our hotel."

"I like the thought of taking out the jet skis," Cass said. "I've seen my parents ride them, but I've never been on one."

"Me neither." Shelby said with a smile. "I guess that settles it. We'll make jet ski rentals our first item of business in the morning."

Katie shouted out in agreement. "Woo hoo! That sounds like fun. I think we're all up for a jet ski race tomorrow. Right, ladies?"

Lisa, along with Alison and Molly, all chimed in about how they were excited to join in as well.

Shelby smiled and nodded. "Good, then I'll go ahead and reserve us six of them first thing tomorrow morning. It looks like they've got a few courses laid out with buoys across the lagoon. According to the map, we can pick out one of the courses and reserve it."

Cass smiled. "That sounds like a lot of fun. I will have to beat you in that race, you know. You're so good at everything else, I have to be able to best you at something."

"You're the best of both of us in many ways, Cass," Shelby said. She leaned over and put her head on Cass's shoulder. Their fingers interlaced and fell onto Cass's lap.

"This has all progressed so fast. I still don't know what I did to deserve you, Shel," Cass whispered. "I didn't think we had a chance to even be friends after that first day. Now we're——" Cass stopped and looked at Shelby. "I always thought I'd find someone new in my life while I was at college. I didn't expect it to happen this way and with you."

"Me neither," Shelby answered. "I guess we're both lucky that we stuck it out after that first day."

"Will you two cut it out," Katie said from the seat behind them. "We'll all be in our rooms soon enough."

"You're such a prude," Lisa said, poking Katie in the ribs from the side. "I don't know what I see in you sometimes."

Katie laughed as she backed away from the tickling fingers. "I know exactly what you see in me. Usually I have to wait for you to get my clothes off to see it, though."

Lisa blushed and all of the others laughed.

Katie smiled and hugged Lisa. "Look who's the prude now."

Cass smiled, listening to the byplay between the other couple. Shelby's friends were all great. They'd accepted Cass without question which made her question if Shelby had told them anything about her background and family. Each of them had at least one implant or enhancement of one sort or another. They each sported v-tats along with a cerebral implant similar to Shelby's to control them.

Cosmetic enhancements like these were quite popular among the more progressive students at the college. Cass still didn't understand why anyone would want to submit to something like that, but she'd come to accept it in Shelby over the last few weeks. She saw these new friends in a similar light.

As she considered the shift in her mindset, it struck Cass how much different her opinion was now when she thought about cyber-humans. She still shuddered at the thought of getting anything done to herself like that, but she didn't begrudge the others for their choices the way she might have at the beginning of the semester.

Checking into the condo took only a few minutes. Lisa had already confirmed their rooms via her connection to the Mantle on the island. Everything was ready and waiting for them. This type of resort was all new to Cass. She'd never stayed in a hotel of any kind before.

When she'd traveled before, her family always stayed in other Sapiens enclaves with local families from the movement. Staying here was very different from staying in someone's home on vacation.

Lisa beamed the room code to everyone's implant so they could get into the room. She asked at the desk for a manual key card for Cass.

"She's not able to process the codes with a cerebral chip. She'll need to open the door herself."

The clerk behind the front desk smiled and nodded. "Of course." She rummaged around in a drawer next to her and then smiled. "Ah ha, here it is. Let me just run this through the reader and get it programmed for you, Miss."

She swiped the chip card and handed it to Cass who slid it into the pocket of her jeans.

"Thank you," Cass said.

"Come on," Shelby said. "Let's go up and check out our rooms. I'll bet it's way nicer than our dorm."

"It'll be nice to have our own bathroom for a change instead of having to share one," Cass remarked. "Some of our neighbors are so gross."

Shelby smiled and reached out to take Cass's hand as they walked to the elevators with the others. When they arrived upstairs and opened the door to the three-bedroom condo facing the beach, Cass marveled at the view out the window. It looked out to the Caribbean Sea beyond the beach below. It was beautiful.

"Shel, this is amazing. I'm so glad you made me come on this trip with you."

Shelby came up behind Cass, wrapping her arms around from behind and hugging her tight. "I'm glad you came. Let's get unpacked in our room, then we can head downstairs. I think we can get drinks at the bar. The drinking age is only eighteen here."

Cass shrugged. She wasn't much of a drinker. Her parents weren't teetotalers but they weren't partiers either. She didn't want to miss out on any of the fun, though. She knew they'd have other things to drink at the bar, too.

After the two got settled in the room, Shelby beamed a message to the others in the group and told them she and Cass were heading down to the pool bar in their suits for a swim and a drink.

Cass didn't have a connected device to listen in on the conversation the way Shelby did. She chatted with all four of the others at once in a group call. It took Cass a moment to realize Shelby wasn't talking to her when she responded from a question from one of the others.

"Yeah, we'll be right down. See you there," Shelby said. She smiled at Cass. "Come on, we can head on down. The others will be there soon."

They both went down to the pool. It resembled a crystal blue river winding around the entire resort. It was nothing like the rectangular backyard swimming pools Cass was used to. She stripped off her t-shirt and shorts revealing her green two-piece suit underneath.

"Very nice," Shelby said, hooking an arm about her waist and pulling her close. "We should go to a tropical paradise more often."

"Stop," Cass said, hugging herself in an unconscious attempt to cover up a little bit. She was not ashamed of her body, but also not used to such a public display of affection from a partner. Shelby had broadened Cass's experiences quite a bit over the last week. When she was in high school, most of her sexual experiences with Susan had been pretty tame and limited.

Shelby stripped down to her suit. It was even skimpier than Cass'. It also revealed the rest of the v-tats on her body. She had one on her upper thigh running from her hip halfway to her knee on the right side. Currently it was a bright image of a spiked Dragon with golden and red scales. Every now and then, its tongue flickered in and out of its mouth followed by a brief burst of flame. Shelby caught Cass staring at her leg. "You like that, Cass? I just downloaded it on the plane. Pretty cool, huh?"

Cass just nodded and smiled. She had to admit, her girlfriend was pretty awesome and nothing like the person Cass expected to end up with.

Shelby ran to the edge of the pool and dove in, surfacing a few yards away and gesturing to Cass. "Come on in, it's perfect."

Cass walked to the edge of the pool and climbed in slowly, lowering herself into the water to chest level. It wasn't too cold at all. Cass dunked her head under and swam out to Shelby in the middle of the crystal, clear water.

After they'd floated around for a few minutes taking in the atmosphere, two of the others arrived at the poolside. Alison, tall with her blonde hair pulled back in a pony tail, and Molly, a tiny girl with short, spiked orange hair walked along the pool deck nearby. Molly waved at them and pointed to the bar at the end of the pool. "Come on. Let's go over to the pool bar and get something to drink."

Alison had already climbed in and headed that way. "Look, they have stools under the water you can sit on."

Cass and Shelby swam over and sat on two of the stools. Cass leaned forward with an elbow atop the bar. She reached for one of the drink menus. The holographic pictures of the fruity drink concoctions intrigued her.

The bartender, a guy only a little older than they, walked over to them from the other side of the bar, where it was dry. He asked in a slow, easy island accent, "What can I get for you ladies?"

"We'll both have a strawberry daiquiri," Shelby said.

"Uh, virgin for me, please," Cass added at the last instant.

"Come on, Cass. You can let your guard down and live a little while you're here."

"I'm living just being here with you, Shel. We don't need me getting drunk on top of it."

Shelby laughed. "I'm not sure. Maybe you'd loosen up a little bit with a few drinks in you. Who knows? You might even end up picking up an enhancement or two while you're down here."

Cass shot Shelby a glance, her eyebrows lowered. "Don't say that. I'll do nothing of the sort."

Shelby started to say something then shook her head and closed her mouth.

The two of them sat in silence for a while, listening to the others chatter around them.

Cass realized her quick denial against any enhancement or implants probably rubbed Shelby the wrong way. It was the last thing that separated the two of them and they still found it to be an awkward subject for conversation.

Cass had told Shelby she accepted her just the way she was, but Cass couldn't help but think Shelby still felt like Cass thought differently of her because of the additions she'd made to her body. It was something she hoped to work through while they were down here together.

"Hey ladies," Katie and Lisa arrived in the pool area and waved from the water's edge.

Shelby's expression lightened as she smiled and waved back. The bartender arrived with their drinks and Shelby and Cass turned on their stools while sipping at their daiquiris.

Shelby pointed at the lounge chairs with their clothes and towels. "Go ahead and put your stuff down there with ours and come on over. The water's great." She lifted her glass. "These are delicious."

Both girls stripped down to their suits and swam over to join Cass, Shelby, Alison, and Molly at the bar. Soon all six of them sat laughing and sipping on their frozen tropical drinks without a care in the world.

Cass wondered how different hers tasted without the alcohol. It was delicious without it but she couldn't help but feel a little left out. She wondered again if she shouldn't have let Shelby order her one just to try. She smiled and decided to try one with alcohol tomorrow after their jet ski outing.

One drink at the bar soon turned into more drinks until Cass was the only sober one sitting there. She perched on her stool and laughed at the antics of the others as they set their drinks down and drifted out into the water to toss a beach ball around. It seemed the game had more to do with splashing each other than catching the ball.

After a bit, Shelby came back over and joined her. The sun was setting over the trees to the west. Shelby raised her hand to get the bartender's attention. "Hey, can we order some food here or do we have to go to the restaurant?"

"I can order something for you," he said. "You'll have to go sit at one of the tables by the pool to eat it. There's a special on jerk chicken and Caribbean fruit salad tonight."

"That'll be awesome," Shelby said. "Order six and send them to that table over there." Shelby pointed to a round table near where all their clothes were laid out on chairs.

The bartender nodded and moved away to place the order.

Cass called out to the others, "Hey, we just ordered dinner for us. It's going to be over there at the table near our stuff."

Alison gave a thumbs-up from the pool just before she was dunked by Molly from behind. Cass laughed at the expression on Alison's face as she went under.

Lisa and Katie slipped up behind Molly and grabbed her by the legs, flipping her over until she went under as well.

Both Molly and Alison surfaced sputtering and spitting water. After a few seconds of gasping, they all fell into another round of laughter and headed for the edge of the pool. Cass slid off her stool and looked at Shelby, "how do we settle up on our bill?"

"Don't worry about it, I attached everything we ordered to our room up here." Shelby tapped the side of her head where her implant was visible by her ear.

"Oh, yeah, I forgot you could do that," Cass said.

"Seriously, Cass, you need to get over it and just get a chip for yourself. You can get one that's completely internal. You'd have access without any external evidence to give you away. Your family would never know."

"You don't know how paranoid people in the enclave are. They have sensors at the gate that detect anyone entering with a connection to the Mantle. All packages get delivered to the gate for scanning before people pick them up on their way in and out. No one without prearranged access is allowed in unless they have a specific invitation from a resident."

Shelby smiled and shook her head. "I can't even imagine what that's like. I suppose police have access, too."

"Only with a warrant. We've had to deal with the harassment of the authorities. Some of them think we're bad people just because we want to live apart."

"You know, Cass, there are people who subscribe to your parents' beliefs that do horrible things to people like me."

Cass nodded. "I've heard rumors about it. Those people are just crazy fringe types. My parents aren't like that, neither is my sister. They may not accept what you've done to your body but that doesn't mean they'd hurt you because of it."

Shelby shrugged. "I guess we'll find out eventually. You know they're going to find out about us at some point. You can't keep me a secret from them forever. What are you going to do when winter break comes and they come to take you home?"

Cass shook her head. She'd been thinking about that since the two of them first kissed. "I don't know. I'll figure something out. I figure I can get away from the enclave often enough to call you at least a couple times a week."

Shelby didn't reply. A sad look crossed her face. She turned and waded the rest of the way to the far side of the pool where the others waited for dinner to arrive. Her departure left Cass alone by the bar.

Cass didn't know what she was supposed to do. She'd told Shelby she cared for her whether her parents did or not. Somehow, Cass got the feeling that wasn't going to be enough for Shelby at some point.

Cass shook her head and put it behind her for now. The waiter had arrived at their table with a tray of food. Maybe dinner would keep Shelby from bringing it up again tonight. Cass waded over to join the others and enjoy the rest of their first night in paradise.

Chapter 7

CASS WOKE up first the next morning. The sun streamed in the window and a chorus of tropical songbirds warbled in the trees outside. It looked like a beautiful day. She turned and leaned over Shelby's sleeping form, curled up next to her.

"Wake up, sleepyhead," Cass crooned in Shelby's ear.

Shelby rolled away from Cass and groaned, pulling the pillow over the top of her head.

Cass laughed. "Come on. You're the one that made the reservation for the jet skis first thing this morning. We need to get some breakfast and then head down to the beach."

"Leave me alone. I feel awful."

"It's your own fault. You kept drinking all night while we were at the club dancing. If you get up and get something to eat and drink, you'll feel better."

Shelby mumbled something unintelligible, sat up, and leaned over with her elbows on her knees. She rested her head in her hands.

"Did you say something?" Cass asked.

"I said, how would you know?" Shelby groaned. "Seriously, you don't drink."

Cass laughed. "I've seen enough holovids to know what happens when you drink too much. Come on, let's go downstairs and get something to eat. We'll all feel a lot better with some food in us. I don't want to be late and miss our time on the jet skis."

Shelby groaned again but got up and changed into her suit then pulled a T-shirt and a pair of shorts on over top. Slipping into her flip-flops, she opened the door. "After you."

Cass smiled and caressed Shelby's face with her fingers as she passed by. Together, they headed down towards the condo entrance. The other four girls surprised Cass. They were already awake and dressed in the living room of the suite.

"Geez, Shel," Katie said. "You look just like I feel."

"Wow, thanks," Shelby said. "I'd make a comment about how you look but everything's a little blurry right now. I'll save it for later."

That set all of them laughing together as they headed out towards the elevators. The doors opened as they arrived, and they all stepped inside and headed down to grab some breakfast on the way to the beach.

Cass enjoyed a hearty breakfast including eggs, bacon, and some sort of spicy island home fries. Everything tasted delicious. The other five women opted for blander buffet options along with mugs of coffee to help them wake up.

The food helped from what Cass could see. Shelby and the others had all perked up by the time they finished breakfast.

Cass checked her watch. "We need to go. It's almost time for our reservation. You all know I'm not going to go easy on you just because you're all hungover."

"Don't worry about us," Shelby said. "I'm ready to take you on." She didn't sound as if she meant it, though.

Cass noticed Shelby didn't have the usual bounce in her step. "Hey, we don't have to do this right now."

"I'll feel better once more of breakfast hits my system," Shelby replied. "The implant uses more blood sugar for power than the rest of my brain. I should have eaten more last night before I went to bed."

Cass laughed. "I'm not sure you could have kept it down. You were pretty far gone by the time we made it back to our room. You're not planning on doing that every night we're here, are you?"

Shelby raised a hand to her forehead with a pained look on her face. "Good Lord, no. That was a bit much even for me."

"I'm glad," Cass said. "I wanted a little attention last night and you were in no condition to give it to me."

Shelby put her arm around Cass's waist. "I promise I'll make it up to you tonight."

"I'll hold you to that," Cass said as they headed out to the beach following the other two couples.

The guy running the jet ski operation on the beach had everything all set up for them. There were six wave riders tied up in the lagoon just beyond where the small swells of waves formed.

Shelby had made the reservation, so she headed over and checked in while Cass and the rest of them put their stuff down and stripped down to their swim suits. Cass kicked off her flip-flops and ran over to where Shelby was chatting with the operator of the concession.

"They're really easy to operate, Miss. You just twist the throttle on the handle to make it speed up, and let go to make it stop. Turn the handle bars left or right to steer."

Shelby nodded. "I'm sure we'll get the hang of it. We have them for the full hour, right?"

"Yes ma'am. I'll come out and flag you down to let you know when your time is almost up. Otherwise, you can just come in whenever you're done before then."

Shelby turned towards the other five girls. "Come on, they're all set and ready to go. We've only got them for an hour, so let's go."

All six of them cheered as they waded out and climbed aboard their jet skis. The operator started and untied the jet skis and gave them all a gentle push towards the center of the lagoon. Soon, all six women raced off through the swells near the shoreline, heading for the calmer water in the center of the lagoon.

As the wind blew through Cass's hair, a shiver of excitement passed down her spine. She'd never done anything like this before and it was the most fun she'd ever had. She hadn't a care in the world and no worries.

For a while, all six of them chased each other around in circles. Then they headed down the beach a distance from where they started. The course marked with bobbing orange buoys gave them obstacles to weave through as they rode.

After they'd been riding and racing for a half hour, Shelby called out and pointed to a rocky outcropping a little farther offshore. It jutted up about fifteen feet in the air from the larger sea swells coming into the lagoon.

Cass saw it and knew what Shelby wanted. She said, "Hey, let's all race from here around that rock and back to the shore. Last one in has to buy us all drinks at the bar later."

Their reply came as a chorus of shouts and trash talk.

Before Cass could do it, Shelby laughed and raised her hand in the air. "Ready?"

"Yes!" Cass yelled out.

The others hooted and hollered their own replies.

Without warning, Shelby pulled her hand down as she yelled in rapid succession, "3-2-1, go."

By the time Shelby said the word go she'd already twisted the throttle all the way with her other hand. Her jet ski took off, getting a big head start on the others.

"Hey, not fair!" Cass yelled. She leaned over the handle bars as she goosed her own throttle and took off after her roommate. She screamed with delight as she chased after Shelby, the wind whistling past her ears.

Cass and the other four girls on the trailing jet skis rode in a tight pack, all jockeying to get in position to try and catch up with Shelby.

They'd closed the distance some by the time Shelby got to the rock. She slowed a little and took the turn a little wide.

Cass saw her chance. She could cut the turn short and beat Shelby around to the other side if she kept her jet ski at full speed.

She was so intent on beating her girlfriend, Cass didn't realize why Shelby had steered wide.

A shelf of rock jutted out from the outcropping just beneath the water. Cass didn't see it until the very last instant.

Too late, she jerked the handle bars to the right to try and avoid the rocks. Despite the last-minute twist to the side, Cass's jet ski hit the submerged ledge at full speed.

She sailed over the handlebars head first, slamming into rocks jutting up from the reef.

Cass's last thoughts consisted of a mix of terror and disappointment. Then, everything went black.

―――――――――――

Chapter 8

―――――――――――

SHELBY SAT in the hospital waiting room, leaning forward with her head in her hands. For the hundredth time she squeezed her eyes shut as the events played over again in her mind.

She still couldn't believe what had happened. The whole accident unfolded in front of her like something out of a holovid horror show.

Shelby didn't realize Cass didn't see the submerged rock until it was way too late to try and warn her. If only she'd thought to pull up and wave her off.

The images played through her mind again.

Cass flew from the jet ski, her arms and legs flailing like a rag doll. She slammed into the rocks headfirst. As her crumpled body slumped down into the waves, Shelby remembered thinking she had to be dead.

Only the quick thinking of Katie and Alison, both nursing students, saved Cass's life.

The two of them jumped off their jet skis and swam over to where Cass floated face down at the base of the rocks. They rolled her over to keep her mouth and nose out of the water.

The rescue squad boat arrived quickly, although it seemed like it took them forever at the time. Shelby knelt nearby on the partially submerged shelf of rock holding onto Cass's outstretched hand as the island rescue paramedics set to work.

There'd been so much blood in the water and all over Cass, Shelby didn't think anything could be done.

The rescue workers kept doing what they could to stabilize Cass. After working to secure her to a floating stretcher and stop the worst of the bleeding, the rescue team lifted Cass out of the water and took off in their rescue boat for the harbor.

Shelby sat alone with the other four women on the rocks as the boat raced away, its siren blaring against the backdrop of seagulls screeching overhead.

By the time Shelby got back to shore with her friends, it was almost an hour after the accident first happened. She raced to the front desk to try and find out where they took Cass.

It took Shelby nearly another hour, with the help of the hotel clerk, to find out where they'd taken Cass and arrange for a boat to the neighboring island where the main hospital was located.

Now all she and the others could do was sit here and wait. When they'd arrived, the nurse at the desk told them the doctors were operating on Cass and they were doing all they could for her.

A clerk came out right after they got there to ask if anyone had any contact information for Cass's family. Shelby looked at the other four then stood up and shrugged, muttering, "No, why?"

"We need to speak to someone about her care. Are you her next of kin or partner?" The woman asked Shelby.

"I guess I'm as close as there is down here," Shelby said, not realizing what she'd agreed to.

The woman held out a tablet for Shelby to sign.

"We just need your consent here to perform life-saving measures as needed."

Shelby considered the form on the tablet for only a few seconds before she signed, unsure what it all meant but wanting them to save Cass no matter what it took.

She sat down to wait with the others again. Shelby probably could've found a contact number for Cass's parents if she'd tried hard enough. They were the legal next of kin but Shelby wasn't in the mood to spring her cyber identity on Cass's parents like that, while telling them their daughter was in a horrible accident. It was better if she waited until she knew something more about her condition.

Shelby knew it was a decision based in part on her own cowardice. She promised herself she'd find a way to contact them after Cass was out of surgery. It didn't matter what they thought of her then.

After sitting with the other four girls in the waiting room for more than four hours, a doctor in pastel green scrubs and a floral cap came out to find them. She was a short woman with dark skin and a set of telescoping ocular implants that Shelby would've thought were pretty cool in any other situation. She supposed they would be super helpful for a surgeon.

The doc came over to them where they sat and asked, "Are you the friends who are here with Cass Armstrong, the girl injured in the jet ski accident?"

Shelby stood up. "Yes, we are. How is she?"

The doctor glanced at the tablet she held and looked up at Shelby. "You're Shelby Moore, her partner?"

"Uh, yes, that's me."

The doctor smiled and said, "She's going to be all right given enough time to recover and adjust. She was very seriously injured. Based on her head injury, we thought we were going to have little chance to save her but we managed to stabilize her. Lucky for her, in the end, our efforts and neural regeneration should restore a good deal of her normal function."

"What do you mean by normal function?" Shelby didn't like the way that sounded for some reason. It triggered something in the back of her mind, something that upset her for some reason.

" Cass's injury happened to come at a time advantageous to her outcome. We recently received some new cerebral cybernetics from the mainland. They are some of the latest gear, which we don't always have on hand. Given the fact that she was on a student trip from the U.S., it was all covered under her student insurance plan."

"What was covered?" Shelby stared at the doctor as it dawned on her what the woman was saying. "You said implants. Did you…?"

"It was the only way we could save her life. She had a severe brain injury and the blow destroyed part of her optic nerve on the right side. We had to do something to retain function or she would have been paralyzed on one side for the rest of her life. We managed to get everything in place in plenty of time for her body to avoid rejection. The nano bots went in and did their work making all the neural connections to the cybernetic core. It'll take her a little while to get used to it, but she'll be all right. After an adjustment period and some therapy, she should be almost as good as new."

"It's not something she ever wanted. She doesn't believe in them." Shelby shook her head. She didn't know what else to say. She wasn't going to yell at the doctor for saving Cassie's life.

"When can we go see her?" Katie asked.

"You can come back two at a time to see her, but only for a few minutes each. If you want, Shelby, you may stay by her side tonight. The nurses don't mind. It might help Cass to see a face she knows when she wakes up later. What she needs most now is rest as the final neural connections are made while she sleeps."

"Thank you, Doctor," Shelby said.

"Not a problem. If you need anything, ask the nurse and I'll be happy to try to get back to you as quickly as possible, otherwise, the residents in the ICU can answer any questions that might come up."

The doctor glanced at the tablet again. "I know you said you're her partner. I don't suppose you have anything to support that, do you?"

"No, I'm sorry. We're on vacation and didn't bring anything like that with us."

"That's all right. We can confirm with her family if you don't. Do you have any contact information for her family? We plan to send a request to the University, but it's after hours so we'll wait until morning."

"You don't have to worry about that, Doctor," Shelby said. "I'll be able to find that for you. They're traveling right now. I don't think the University has their current information updated."

"All right, I'll tell my clerk to remove the query from her to-do list. Make sure you get that to me right away when you find it. You can find me in the hospital directory over the net."

"Thank you again, Doctor."

The doctor walked away and Shelby turned to the other girls.

"Did she say they gave Cass an implant?" Alison asked. "Isn't she going to be super pissed about that?"

Shelby shrugged, then sighed and nodded. "Probably, but they had to save her life, right?"

"It must've been pretty serious if they did it without asking anyone's permission," Lisa said.

Shelby thought back to what she'd signed earlier when the clerk mistook her for Cass's partner. She pushed the thought from her mind. All that mattered was that Cass was alive.

Katie nodded to the hallway the doctor came from. "Maybe we should go back and see what they did to her. It sounded like they did a pretty extensive upgrade."

Shelby looked at her friends and then at the door to the rest of the hospital. "Do you all mind if I go up by myself first? Then I'll come down and you guys can go up, too."

"Of course. You go," Alison said. "In fact, why don't you just stay up there? The four of us will head back to the hotel. Just send us updates when you hear anything. There's no sense all of us hanging out here in the hospital all weekend."

Shelby smiled and said, "I agree. Don't waste the weekend. She's asleep right now anyway. I'll make sure I keep you up-to-date with what's going on. I should be able to message you all through the night."

The four girls each hugged Shelby and left her in the waiting room. She turned towards the corridor the doctor indicated leading to the intensive care unit.

Shelby took a deep breath and walked down the hallway following the signs until she reached a bank of elevators. She pressed the button to go up and waited for the next elevator car.

She had no idea what she was going to say to Cassie when she awakened. There was no way to predict what her reaction was going to be when she found out about what the doctors had done to save her life.

The only thing Shelby knew was it probably wasn't going to be positive. All she could do was be there when Cass figured it out. The news would devastate her.

When the elevator doors opened on the second floor, there was a desk with a clerk straight ahead of her. Behind the clerk, in a circular space, nurses scurried all around through open doorways situated around the central office station.

The clerk smiled as Shelby approached. "Hi, can I help you? Are you here to see a family member?"

"Uh, yes, I am. I'm here to see my girlfriend Cass Armstrong? The doctor said she's here."

"She just arrived. The nurses are still getting her situated in her bed. I'll have her nurse come out and get you as soon as she's ready for you to come see her."

Shelby nodded and looked around. She didn't want to go back downstairs to the waiting room. She spotted a few chairs next to the elevator doors.

Shelby hooked her thumb over shoulder at the chairs. "Is it all right if I sit over here?"

"Sure, honey. Go sit down. As I said, the nurse will be out very soon."

Shelby walked over and sat down, watching the buzz of activity in the busy intensive care unit. The nurses and their assistants all seemed to be working on doing something all the time. They never stopped.

She spotted two people, a man and a woman, in longer lab coats. She figured they must be the doctors who worked alongside the nurses to care for the patients here. Unlike the nurses, they stayed behind the counter at their desks most of the time.

The whole scene fascinated her. While she'd settled on a psych major, part of her had considered becoming a nurse especially after Alison and Katie told her how much they enjoyed the program.

This was her first time inside a hospital. Seeing all this made her think that all the action takes place in a hospital.

Shelby pictured what it would be like for her in that role someday. It felt like a good fit.

She was still lost in her thoughts when a nurse from the facility came over to her. "Are you Cass's friend?"

"Yes, I am," Shelby said as she stood. "I'm Shelby. Is she all right? Can I see her now?"

"Of course, you can. My name is Hildi. I'll be her nurse from now until tomorrow morning. You can sit with Cass all night if you want."

"I would like that," Shelby said as she followed Hildi back to one of the individual rooms.

"On the overnight shift, we're pretty relaxed around here. After I show you where Cass's room is, I'll show you where we keep drinks and snacks for families and patients. Feel free to help yourself if you plan on staying here tonight."

Shelby nodded, trying to take it all in as Hildi led her to one of the glass-walled rooms off the central desk area.

Cass's room had a glass sliding door facing in towards the center of the unit. Shelby stopped at the door and stood there, suddenly rooted to the spot. Her first view of Cass in the bed rocked her to her core.

Cass had all sorts of tubes and wires hooked to her. There seemed to be some sort of metal fabric mesh encircling the top of her head. White bandages peeked out from beneath the mesh covering.

Shelby figured the wire mesh was some sort of monitor for the implants. She scanned Cass's body as she lay in the bed. Aside from some bumps and bruises on the rest of her body, most of the injury to her girlfriend centered around the right side of her face and head.

Peeking out from under the mesh bonnet, a shiny silver metal implant extended from the edge of Cass's cheek next to her right eye all the way back to her ear, arching up and over the upper lobe and down behind it.

Shelby tried to figure out what the implant might do in addition to repairing her lost brain function. The doctor had said they had some of the latest models from the States.

"Hildi, exactly what do all the implants she received do? How extensive was the replacement work?"

"I just got a quick look at her chart, but it appears they had to do quite a bit." Hildi moved around to the other side of the bed and typed something onto the screen of the monitor hanging on the wall.

She kept talking as she worked on getting Cass situated. "I'm still getting up to speed on all the details, but it looks like they did a full replacement of her right eye and optic nerve. That includes an ocular implant matched to her existing eye. They also inserted a temporal cerebral magnifier to help retain her memory and function from the portion of her brain that was damaged."

"How much of her memory was affected?" Shelby became frightened about the possibility Cassie might not remember her.

"We won't know for sure until she wakes up. However, based on the quick report I saw, they were able to salvage quite a bit from the synaptic relays they had to replace. I think it's hopeful that she will only be missing some of her short-term memory and possibly a few other items here and there from her long-term memory. The implant should compensate for a lot of that over time, though."

Shelby nodded and walked over to stand beside the bed. She reached out and held Cass's hand. Her fingers felt cold. With her other hand, Shelby reached up and adjusted the blanket, pulling it up higher on Cass's chest.

Hildi noticed what she did. "Don't worry, we'll get her warmed up again. They keep the surgical suite cold all the time on purpose. It helps the patients during brain surgery. It's always a shock to the family when they come up here and see someone just afterward. The patients always feel so cold when they first get here."

"Oh, okay. Thanks for letting me know. Um, is there anything I can do to help? I don't want to be in your way, but I'd like to help take care of her, too?"

Hildi smiled. "Of course you can. Why don't you sit down there next to her. I have to go out and add some notes to her chart. I'll be just outside the door. If you want to sit and hold her hand and keep an eye on her while I tend to the admin stuff that would be great. It probably won't be long before she wakes up, maybe only an hour or two. When an implant like this is put in, the whole healing process is accelerated by the nano bots we inject."

Shelby smiled. It felt good to be able to help in some way. She sat down in the chair beside the bed and gave Cass's hand a gentle squeeze. Hildi left to tend to her other duties while Shelby sat and waited for Cass to wake up.

"I'm here for you, Cassie, honey. I'm here."

Chapter 9

CASS PULLED with her arms as she swam through the deep blue water towards the dim sunlight above. She struggled to reach the surface before she ran out of air.

The sunlight beamed down. She could see it glimmering through the water above her. All she had to do was kick and pull until she broke the surface. It couldn't be too much farther, could it?

Despite fighting with all her strength, Cass couldn't get there. The harder she fought to emerge, the longer it seemed to take.

Frustration and anger at not being able to break through made her redouble her efforts.

She would not be denied.

Cass pushed harder against the water around her, kicking with all her might.

It never occurred to her why she hadn't drowned already. She'd already been underwater for so long.

Cass continued to fight against the pull of the current sucking her down. After what felt like hours of exhausting time struggling against the current towards day, she finally broke through and pushed into the sunlight.

In the hospital room, Cass's eyelids fluttered open for the first time in more than a day. She didn't move at first. She just stared at the white ceiling above her trying to understand where she was.

Cass raised her right hand and saw wires and a clear plastic tube attached to her arm. She realized she was in a hospital room or medical suite of some kind. Cass tried to sit up, but when she tried to move, her left shoulder and arm felt like lead weights and held her body down. Her whole left side felt heavy and numb.

"Wh—where am I?" Cass said. Her voice sounded hoarse and raspy as if she hadn't spoken for a long time.

A familiar voice nearby answered her.

"Oh, my God. Cass, you're awake." Shelby's face came into view as she leaned over the hospital bed. "I'm so glad you woke up. We were all so worried about you."

Cass stared at Shelby for a long time before answering. There was something strange about the way her girlfriend looked. The lines around her face were sharper, and in some ways more colorful. There were fine details she could see that she'd never seen before. It was almost as if there was a sort of aura all around Shelby.

"Am I in the hospital? How did I get here?"

"Do you remember the accident on the jet skis? We were racing and you ran into some rocks. They rushed you here to the hospital. The doctors saved your life." Shelby paused. "It was bad, Cassie. Really bad."

"Injured, how?" Cass asked. She still felt a little numb every-where, mostly on her left side. Her head ached a little, too.

"You hit your head when you landed on the rocks," Shelby said, continuing her description as tears filled her eyes. "I thought you were dead."

Cass didn't understand why Shelby seemed to be hesitating to give a full answer. And why was she crying?

Frustrated with the delay, Cass blurted out, "Shelby just tell me. I don't understand why you're holding back. What aren't you telling me?"

"Cass, it's not just that you were injured. Like I said, you almost died. The doctors here had to save your life and they had to do, uh, well, some things to make sure you lived."

Something about the way Shelby answered frightened Cass, though she couldn't say why exactly. "What do you mean, Shelby? What did they do to me?"

Shelby reached down and held Cass's right hand in both of hers. Cass glanced down, seeing Shelby's metallic hand and real hand wrapped around her own. Once again, the image she saw looked strange and alien to her.

As Cass looked back up at her girlfriend's face, tears streamed down her cheeks.

"Shelby, why are you crying? I feel pretty much fine. I don't understand."

"Cass, they had to put in an implant to save your brain and your eye and some other stuff."

At first, Cass didn't understand what Shelby said. "An implant?" She couldn't wrap her mind around it. She would never have allowed such a thing to happen. Surely Shelby knew that by now?

"Yeah, Cass, multiple implants. They're on the right side of your head and face. From your eye back."

Cass groaned and focused her strength to lift up her right hand. She found she had more control of her right side now and pulled her hand away from Shelby's grasp. She reached up and touched the side of her face with her fingertips. She winced at the tenderness of the skin around her eye and cheek. Then her fingers touched something hard. It wasn't cold. It was warm; like Shelby's metal hand.

Panic set in for Cass right away. Her breathing increased as she traced her fingers along the metal surface, running her fingers in a line from next to her right eye all the way back and over her ear. She continued tracing the edge of the metal thing on her face until her fingers returned back to where they started just behind her eye.

"Oh my God, oh my God, oh my God, what did they do to me?"

"Cass, it's not that bad. They saved your life and it really isn't that much."

"You said they replaced my eye. But I can see you. Nothing's changed." Cass blinked several times to prove her point.

Shelby smiled down at her, wiping away tears so they didn't fall on Cass. "It looks fine. They did a good job matching your eye color."

This was wrong, all wrong. They had to come out.

Cass dug at the skin around the metal implant in the side of her skull, digging her fingernails in to try and pry it out. She winced at the pain but redoubled her efforts to scrape at the edge of the metal band. "Get this thing out of me, Shelby. I can't have an implant. I won't be me anymore. I won't be human."

The day nurse came rushing in from outside the room. She snapped an order at Shelby. "Pull her arm away and hold it down. We can't let her injure herself. We have to stop her until she gets used to the implants."

"Nurse," Cass called out. "You don't understand. You have to get these things out of me. I can't have implants. I can't have these things in my head."

"Cass, honey. My name is Merry. I'm here to help you. You need to take some deep breaths. I know it's a lot to process, so don't think about anything at all, just look at my face and take deep breaths with me. I'll count along with you as breath in and out."

Cass looked at the nurse and watched her open her mouth to breathe and count along with her. Despite the overwhelming panic sweeping through her, Cass realized after a few seconds she was following the nurse's instructions.

Soon, her breathing slowed down as she tried to match the nurse's pace and rhythm. Merry continued her steady encouragement while Cass calmed down.

Once her breathing settled down, Merry smiled and reached up to stroke her hair. "That's much better. It's not unusual for someone in your situation to have a reaction like that. Everything is so new right now and you're still adjusting to the neural interface."

As Merry stroked her hair and Shelby held on to her hand, Cass's thoughts shifted through several things. She wondered about the hair on the right side where they put in the implant.

"My hair on the right side. Did they shave it off?"

Merry nodded. "Just a little bit of it. They needed to in order to make sure they could put everything right, but it'll grow back and be good as new before you know it. They've given you some follicle stimulating medicine to speed up the regrowth."

"It looks pretty rad, actually," Shelby added.

Cass struggled to tamp down her panic again. She had to think this through. She could find a way out of this if she took her time. "Can I get a mirror? I need to see."

"Sure," Merry said. "I thought you might want that and put one here by the bed. Here."

Merry held up a square mirror with a white plastic handle, angling it so Cass could see the right side of her face and head.

Cass turned her face to see better. The swelling around that side of her face made everything look puffy and bruised.

"Can I have my hand back, Shel?"

"Sure," Shelby replied, releasing her hold on Cass's right hand.

Cass lifted her hand again and traced her finger tips along the silver and gray metal plate running from her eye to her ear. She felt the smooth, polished surface glide by under her fingers as she touched the implant.

Questions swirled through her brain. Most importantly: How was she going to live with something like this in her brain? The Mantle would take her over and she'd cease to be herself anymore. It was just like she'd learned in all the horror stories they told her as she grew up.

As she asked herself the questions, the panic returned.

Shelby reached over and took Cass's hand again to keep her from digging at the implant. "Cass, settle down. Come on, breathe with me like you did with Merry. Look into my eyes and breathe along with me. You can do this. It's all going to be all right."

Cass once again focused on the voice and tried to pull her thoughts away from the machine inside her head. This time Shelby talked her down and she found herself calming much more quickly.

Merry moved to get something from a shelf by the door. She picked up a metal syringe and attached it to the tubing going into Cass's left arm. She pushed the plunger down. Cass watched as the pale blue liquid ran through the intravenous tubing into her arm.

"What's that? What are you doing to me?" Cass asked.

"It's just another dose of nano bots," Merry replied. "You need them right now to keep your body from rejecting any of the new additions. Eventually, everything will settle down as the neural-cerebral interface completes all the connections. Then your own system will stop your body from rejecting things. Don't worry. We'll have that all balanced out before you leave."

Cass's mind swam as more thoughts raced through what the nurse told her. Now she had tiny robots roaming in her body, all connected to the Mantle, all trying to change her even more. She'd never be herself again. How was she going to begin to tell her parents about this? They would never forgive her.

Before she could get herself worked up again, Cass grew tired and everything slowed down.

"I feel weird, sleepy."

"That's normal," Merry said. "The bots sedate you so they can do their work in peace. You go back to sleep, hon. You'll feel much better when you wake up next time. The medicine I added to the nano bot injection will help keep you calm when you awaken again."

Cass tried to say something. She heard her own voice in the distance. "Don't like the implants. Don't want to be a sub."

As Cass drifted off to sleep, Shelby blinked to fight back tears.

Shelby had never heard Cass use the word sub before when referring to anyone with an enhancement, let alone herself. It spoke volumes about how deeply her prejudices were seeded regarding the things she learned growing up. Now she feared herself.

Shelby let go of Cass's hand and got up. She needed to take a walk and process her thoughts. She'd been here in the ICU for almost twenty-four hours.

Merry stood at the nurses' station chatting with another one of the ICU staff members. She looked up as Shelby came out of Cass's room. "Going to take a break?"

"Yeah, I just need to clear my mind a little bit."

"It's all right. Cass is going to be fine. She just had a bad reaction to everything. It's a lot to take in all at once."

"Yeah, I guess so. How much of what she said in there is her and how much is the meds talking, though?"

Merry smiled. "It's mostly the meds, along with her injury and fear talking. Don't take anything she says over the next few days personally. She's got to adjust and find her own way through this. The best thing you can do is to be there with her as she works it out."

Shelby nodded. It was good advice in general, though she wondered if Cass would ever get over having implants of her own.

"Oh, one more thing," Merry said. She pointed to the tablet she held. "Were you able to find her parents' contact information? We really need to reach out and notify them. The university got back to us with their names listed but not the contact info. I tried to do a search on the Mantle but it came up empty."

"Um, I don't have it yet, but I can try again to get it. In the midst of all the action and then Cass waking up, I totally forgot." Shelby hoped Merry couldn't tell she had lied. She didn't want Cass's parents finding out about this, at least not now. It would be up to Cass to decide whether to tell them, although how she was going to hide it from them was a mystery to Shelby.

"I'm getting ready to go off shift," Merry said. She gestured to the woman she was speaking with. "This is Jess. She'll be taking over for me for the next twelve hours. She can help you with anything you need when you get back from your walk."

Jess smiled at Shelby and nodded. Shelby returned the smile, though she didn't feel it inside right now. She had a lot she had to process and figure out. Shelby feared what Cass would do to herself when she woke up next time. They couldn't keep sedating her. There had to be a way to help Cass get through this without mutilating herself in the process.

Shelby turned and headed for the elevators. Maybe if she went downstairs and got a bite to eat in the cafeteria, she might feel better.

As she waited for the elevator, she dialed up a connection via her implant and fired off a few quick messages to their friends back at the resort. They'd all left Shelby messages wondering how things were going.

She didn't tell them anything about Cass's bad reaction. She only said Cass woke up but was now back to sleep. It was better if they didn't know about what Cass said about herself and indirectly about others like the rest of them.

Shelby stepped into the elevator when it opened and took it downstairs to the first floor. It was time for her to come up with a plan to get Cass back to school without her parents finding out about what happened. They were going to have to have a plan in place if she was going to help Cass get through this.

Chapter 10

CASS GROANED and stretched as she woke up. Immediately she regretted trying to work her stiff muscles. She realized they weren't just taut… she felt battered and bruised all over.

She'd had the most horrible dream. She'd lived through a horrible experience right out of her childhood nightmares.

Cass thought about how vivid and real the dream had been. It was silly, really. She remembered it all. She woke up in a hospital bed after having cybernetic implants forced into her brain.

As she tried to recall the nightmare, her mind wandered back to how sore her body felt. She had a horrifying realization.

It was all real.

Cass opened her eyes and gasped. Where was everybody? A large glass window and an open sliding door revealed people in hospital scrubs busily moving about. *Oh, God.*

As more memories returned, her hand slid up toward the side of her face. *No, no, no...please, no.*

Her fingertips traced the contour of her cheek, moving over her skin until it reached a hard, unyielding ridge that ran from beside her eye back over her ear along the side of her head.

Cass didn't try to dig at it and remove it this time. Her head and thoughts were clearer now. She knew that wasn't possible. It would take another surgery to remove it.

She squeezed her eyes shut and tried to force herself not to cry. There had to be a way to fix this. She would find a way to have whatever implants the butchers put inside her removed. It was the only way she could restore herself, her humanity.

Opening her eyes again with a newly found sense of purpose, Cass looked over to her left side and spotted a small wire cord attached to her bed rail with a clip. There was a red button at the end of it.

She reached up to grab it and pressed the button with her thumb.

About thirty seconds later, a woman came into the room. She didn't seem much older than Cass herself and wore pastel pink scrubs.

"Hi, Cassie. I'm Jess, your nurse today. I see you finally woke up again. Are you feeling a little better this time? Merry told me you had some trouble before. Are you doing all right?"

As she talked and asked Cass questions, Jess walked around her bed and checked some things on the monitor hanging on the wall to the left. She turned back to smile down at Cass in the bed.

"I need to talk to my doctor," Cass said. "I need to talk to whoever it was that did this to me."

"I'll have to see if your surgeon is on site today," Jess said. "He works at other hospitals here in the islands. I can have one of the ICU residents come in and talk to you if that will help. They're the doctors on call right now. Will that be all right?"

"Yes, please. I have a lot of questions I need to ask them."

"All right, I'll be right back. After you talk to them, we can see about getting you up out of bed and walking around a bit."

While she waited for the doctor to come, Cass spotted a plastic cup and straw sitting next to her bed. She reached out with her left hand and picked it up. Her hand and arm trembled so much as she brought the cup over to have a sip, she was afraid she'd spill it. Luckily, the lid stayed in place.

Cass savored the feel of the cold water in her parched mouth.

The cool liquid felt good going down her raspy, dry throat, too. She took a few more sips while she waited.

She set the cup down as another woman came into the room. She wore a long, white lab coat over her scrubs.

Cass tried to push herself upright in the bed to speak to the doctor. She groaned as her aching muscles betrayed her and she decided to remain as she was.

"Hi, Cass. I'm Dr. Henderson," the woman said in a voice with a smooth island lilt. "Jess said you had a few questions for me. Here, let me help you sit up a little bit. I think that will be more comfortable for you, am I right?"

"Yes, that would be nice," Cass said.

The doctor reached over and pressed a button on the side rail. The head of the bed started to tilt upward to a steeper angle. Cass felt silly as she realized she could have helped herself sit up all along. This was all so new to her.

After Dr. Henderson helped her sit up, she smiled at Cass and said, "So, what kind of questions can I answer for you?"

"I want to know how long I have to have these implants in my head?"

"I don't understand, Cass. What do you mean how long?"

"I mean, when can I have them removed? I want them taken out as soon as possible."

The doctor's brow creased as a puzzled look crossed her face. "Cass, I don't think you understand. There is no way we can remove these implants, ever. The surgeon literally saved your life by putting them in place. They have to remain or you'll die. I was here when you were brought in to the trauma center. You suffered a severe traumatic head injury when you struck that rock. Vital portions of your brain were failing. There is no way to remove it without you dying. If the implants were removed, you would suffer severe mental and physical impairment requiring lifelong hospitalization."

"What do you mean by impaired. How impaired would I be?"

"I'd have to consult with the staff neurologist and have them look over the extent of the brain damage you suffered, as well as what we would have to do to remove the implant. Based on what I do know, though, it is my belief you'd be paralyzed on one side and probably lose a large portion of your mental faculties."

When Cass didn't say anything, Dr. Henderson continued. "Your memory, perhaps even your ability to speak or understand language would be lost. It's hard to say for sure. Even with our modern advancements and ability to interface with the neurons in the human brain, we still do not fully understand the process the brain uses to connect everything together. It's one of the main things that separate us from artificial intelligences. They are hampered by these limitations. Robots with AI interfaces have to use the Mantle network to navigate and move about simply because they do not possess the raw processing power or capability for filtering all the data our brains do."

"If that's so, how does this thing in my head make me better? If it can't do the things my brain can do, why is it something that can help me?"

"Only a portion of your brain was injured. Hasn't anyone gone over the extent of your injuries with you?"

Cass shook her head. "I just woke up."

Dr. Henderson sighed. "Let's start with the injuries that were most severe. When you struck the rock, you hit the front and right side of your head. This caused significant trauma to the cerebral cortex and frontal lobe of your brain as well as severing the right optic nerve. Your right eye itself and some core sense of your ability to hear and comprehend processed information from that side were lost as well."

The doctor continued. "The implants you have replaced the need for the damaged areas to continue functioning. We were able to download most of your memories from the damaged tissue before it died. Your cybernetic interface restored the bulk of the memories from the lost tissue as far as we can tell. You may find gaps as time goes by, but most of them will fill in eventually as you rebuild neural connections with the memory in your implant. Your optic nerve and eye were replaced with a cybernetically enhanced one. You'll find that you can see things a lot better from that side. You have a variety of options to choose from to utilize the full capabilities of the ocular implant."

"What kind of capabilities?"

"You'll have nearly perfect night vision. You can also see in the infrared and ultraviolet spectrums, as well as possess the ability for some limited telephoto enhancement. You have standard image and video capture capabilities as well. Essentially, you'll be able to zoom in on things at a distance, see them as if they were close up, and even record them if you want. All of this will take time to develop. The implant's systems will open access to the full capabilities as it senses your successful management of what is currently available. Basically, your brain needs to learn how to control what's there before new things are added. It will take some time to return to full capability."

Something the doctor said clicked for Cass. "I don't have time. What day is it? I need to get out of this hospital. When can I leave?"

"It's Sunday. It's the day after your accident."

"I have to return home tomorrow. I have to get back to the school before my parents find out what happened to me. They'll never understand this. They won't understand me at all anymore."

"Cass, I'm sure your parents will love you just the same. If you want, I can talk to them for you. You're not a different person. We just had to fix part of you, that's all."

Cass shook her head. The doctor had no idea what her parents would or would not accept in her. "No, you can't tell them anything. You haven't called them, have you?"

"No, as a matter of fact, that's one of the things I wanted to ask you. Your friend hasn't been very helpful with giving us information about how to reach them. Can you give me a net address or number where they can be reached?"

A wave of relief passed over her. Thank God Shelby had watched out for her and kept them from contacting her parents.

"Please don't contact anyone about my condition. If I tell you no, you won't, right?"

"You're an adult, Cass. We can't force you to tell your family if you don't want to. Is there something you're not telling me? Do you not feel safe at home?"

It was a strange question to ask and before the accident, Cass wouldn't have hesitated answering. Home was the safest place she knew.

Except, it wasn't anymore.

"I'm fine. I just want this all kept private. I really need to go back tomorrow with my friends. I have to get back to school."

"Cass, I must advise against that. This is not something you can just bounce back from. The nano bots and our quick-heal treatments after surgery will treat all the physical injuries in just a few days. Your brain and implants are another matter. You need to take time to adjust to everything. It might take a few weeks for you to fully integrate with the new systems installed in your brain."

"I don't have two weeks. I have to get out of here now." Cass started to push herself up higher in the bed while she pushed and pulled up the side rail that fenced her in the bed. Dr. Henderson reached out and gently pulled her hand away from the rail.

"Cass, let's talk about this. If you really insist on leaving early, I can't keep you here. I suppose, if I must, I can refer you to a facility back in the United States. We could send your medical records there and you could travel home and check in at the facility once you're back. That's the best I can do. I still advise against it, but if you have to leave, I can't legally stop you."

Cass stared straight ahead at the wall and tried to organize her thoughts. It was like trying to see in the distance on a foggy day. She knew she had to get out of here. If she promised to do what the doctor asked, it sounded as if they'd let her go early.

"Dr. Henderson, I would like to check out tomorrow and be released. I'll follow your instructions and check in at a facility at home when I'm back. You can send all the medical records with me on a chip. I will give them to a facility near my university when I arrive home."

Dr. Henderson paused as if trying to gauge Cass's response.

Cass had always been a horrible liar. She worried Dr. Henderson saw through her deception. She had no intention of going through with any extended therapy that would keep her out of school. Her parents would surely find out about it if she did.

The doctor nodded. "All right, Cass. I'll start getting the orders together for your discharge. I'll make a final decision tomorrow depending on how you're doing in the morning. First things first, though, we need to get you out of this bed and walking a little bit before I'll even consider letting you go. Let's see how you do moving around here in our unit before I determine if it's going to be acceptable to let you go home."

Cass nodded and Dr. Henderson smiled.

"Excellent. I'll tell Jess what we have planned and she can come help you get up out of this bed."

The doctor left the room and Cass was alone with her thoughts. There was so much she had running through her brain.

For a moment, she wondered if her thoughts were her own anymore. What if her thoughts were influenced by the cybernetic circuits in her brain rather than her own ideas? There was so much she didn't know. She wished Shelby were here. She might be able to answer Cass's questions.

Jess returned to the room with a big grin on her face. "The doctor says we need to get you out of that bed. That is great news. I always believe it's best to get people up and walking as quickly as possible. After all, moving around on your own makes you feel normal again."

"I remember a friend of mine was here earlier. Do you know where she is?"

"I do. You must mean Shelby. She's a very nice girl. I got the impression from her that you and she are very close."

Cass nodded. "We are. Is she still here at the hospital?"

"I believe so. I think she just went to get something to eat. She'll be back up on the unit shortly. Why don't we surprise her and get you up and moving. Maybe when she gets back, you'll be sitting in that chair over there rather than up here in the bed. Does that sound like a good idea?"

Cass nodded. Anything was better than being stuck in this bed any longer than she had to be. She was determined to work as hard as she could to give the doctors no excuse to keep her in the hospital past tomorrow.

Her parents would be calling in a few days when she was supposed to be back in her dorm. They'd ask about the trip. Cass had to be back in her room when they did. Somehow, she'd figure out a way to hide what happened from them.

Chapter 11

CASS CAME BACK from her brief walk around the nurses' station with one of the nurse's aides. Together with Jess, the aide helped her sit in a padded chair at the end of her bed.

Cass leaned back and reached up to touch the side of her face. She winced when she pressed too hard. There were no bandages anymore, which amazed her.

"How's it feel, honey?" Jess asked.

"It hurts a little. I don't understand. How did you do the surgery with no bandages?"

"We only put bandages on wounds for a day or so now unless there's a reason to keep the wound open. Otherwise, after surgery, we use a dermal regenerator, quickheal, and nano bots to help the skin grow back. In cases where we have put in an implant like yours, there is a dermal regeneration strip encircling the perimeter of the implant. It adheres to your skin so it is always tight up against the side of the device, keeping things sealed. After the swelling goes down, there won't be any scarring at all.

Cass felt a small shudder every time the nurse mentioned the implant. She still had a hard time adjusting to the concept of having one of those things in her head.

Once again, she worried if she wasn't thinking like herself anymore. Was this how the machines fooled people into thinking they were normal? Cass still felt like herself and had all the memories she thought she should. Of course, she wouldn't know if anything was missing, would she?

"Why the frown, Cass?" Shelby asked from the doorway to her room. "I leave for an hour or so and come back to find out you've been up and walking around without me. How are you?"

Cass caught herself smiling for the first time in a long time when she saw Shelby standing there. She winced a little as the smile pulled at the taut skin of her swollen face. She also remembered her reaction when she first woke up.

"I was just thinking about how things change so quickly. I don't know if I'm me or not anymore." Her hand drifted up to touch the implant again.

"Don't worry about that," Shelby said as she walked over and sat down on the end of Cass's bed next to the chair. Shelby looked over at the nurse. "Jess, do you mind if I talk to her alone for a little bit? I can call you if we need anything. I know you're very busy."

"Absolutely," Jess said with a smile. "You let me know if you need anything. I'll be right outside."

Both of them waited for the nurse to leave before saying anything.

Shelby bent down and kissed Cass's forehead. "You almost died, Cass. I can't believe I almost lost you."

"I'm not sure you haven't. Are you sure I'm still me, Shel?"

Shelby frowned. "Stop that. Do you think that way about me? Do you think my feelings for you are fake because of my implants?"

Cass shook her head.

Shelby continued. "Don't let your family and the things they told you growing up poison you against yourself. You've got other problems to deal with right now without giving yourself extra headaches."

"My family situation is my biggest problem right now, Shelby. I can't go home. I can't go home ever again."

Shelby shook her head. "I know you think your parents will

disown you or something. I can't imagine they would take the chance and lose you over something like this, though. It wasn't even your fault. How could they blame you?"

"It's not about blame," Cass said. "It's about optics. At least I know that's what my father would say. He has to keep up appearances for his work. How can he stay active advising people like Sterling Noble when he has a daughter who everyone thinks is a freak?"

"Stop it, Cassie. You're not a freak. Do you think I'm a freak?"

Cass stopped, considering what her girlfriend said. She shook her head. "No, you're not a freak. You're the best thing that ever happened to me."

Cass reached out and grasped Shelby's hand.

Shelby squeezed back. "Damn straight I am. Don't you forget it."

She reached over with her other hand to run her fingers along the side of Cass's face next to the implant. "I know you're worried about who you are and how you look right now. I think it looks pretty awesome, though. Have you tried accessing the Mantle or the local net yet?"

A stab of panic struck Cass. "I hadn't even thought about it. I'd be scared to even try it."

"They probably haven't switched on all the accessibility features yet since you're still getting used to it. I suppose the system is still installing the connections and routines required to keep things running and transmitting signals to the rest of your brain."

Cass reached up and brushed Shelby's hand away. Having her girlfriend touch the implant made her self-conscious.

"I guess the eye is working," Cass said. "Things don't look normal. The doctor said I can see things in the infrared and ultraviolet ranges."

"That's awesome," Shelby said. "I'll bet you can see in the dark. All my enhancements are just for cosmetic purposes. Even my arm isn't juiced up to make me super strong or anything. It's just there for effect and to make sure I always have all the cool tools and stuff."

Shelby held her metal hand up and wiggled her fingers as different implements and tools extended from them.

Cass always smiled when Shelby did that. It had the same effect now.

"What else did the doctor tell you?" Shelby asked. "Do you have any other capabilities that come along with the implants?"

Cass shrugged. "I guess there's some other things that'll show up over time as my brain gets used to interfacing with everything. She seems to feel most of the implant's capabilities so far revolve around capturing and restoring my memories. I don't feel like I've forgotten anything but she told me that there will be some holes in what I can and cannot remember."

Shelby nodded and smiled. "It's all right. If you don't remember something, I'll help you. I can remember for you."

The statement from Shelby reassured Cass a little, even though she didn't want to deal with the implant at all. She still had trouble wrapping her mind around the fact she was stuck like this forever. Having Shelby around was going to be critical in how she adjusted to everything.

"If you want," Shelby said. "I can see if you're allowed to eat anything. I bet they haven't fed you at all."

Cass shook her head. "No, and now that you mention it, I am suddenly super hungry."

"Let me go out and chat with Jess. I'll see what they have that you can eat. They probably don't have any trays for lunch yet because it's early, but they have snacks and things like that."

Shelby left the room to go track down Jess and some food. Cass watched her leave. As she did, she tried to focus just on her right eye, concentrating on the different types of images her brain was attempting to filter from the ocular implant.

All of the sudden, Shelby's image changed from vibrant full color to a grayscale black-and-white. It shocked Cass. For a second or two, she thought she'd broken something. Right away, she tried thinking of colors, though, and it switched back.

She wondered what else she could do. Cass began trying to

adjust the image in her right eye using trial and error while she waited for Shelby to come back.

By the time her girlfriend returned, Cass had figured out how to not only change from color to black-and-white images and back, but also how to adjust the spectrum sensitivity to only infrared or ultraviolet light sources.

It was fun to play with the settings. She could even read some parts of the electromagnetic spectrum as she watched waves of energy coming off some of the equipment around the nurses' station in the center of the ICU.

Shelby came back into the room and stopped, smiling. "You have the silliest little grin on your face. What are you doing?"

"Oh, nothing," Cass said. She felt her face heat up and realized she was blushing.

"Tell me," Shelby urged. "You were up to something. Did you discover X-ray vision or something?"

"Close," Cass said with a laugh. "I was trying to figure out how my new eye worked. I managed to figure out a few different settings that change the way things look when I concentrate on them."

"You don't really have something like x-ray vision, do you?" Shelby asked. "I don't want you undressing any of those cute nurses out there. You've got me for that kind of thing, remember?"

Shelby's hint at jealousy made Cass laugh. She was never the jealous one of the two of them. Cass always worried about people who might be attracted to Shelby, not the other way around.

"Did you get me any food?"

"Yeah, I found some stuff in the break room. They have a refrigerator in there for patients with juice along with some crackers and cookies. I checked with Jess. She will be right in with some things to hold you over until lunch gets here. You've been put on a normal diet so you'll probably be able to eat whatever they bring up."

"Awesome, because I think I can eat a horse right now."

Jess overheard her as she walked into the room with a cup full of juice and a couple packets of peanut butter crackers. "I heard that. It's good that you're hungry. The more you eat, the faster everything will heal up on the inside. We can use a dermal generator to close up the skin around wounds, but the adjustment to the internal wounds takes a little longer to heal. The more you eat good food, especially protein, the better and faster you'll heal."

She set the food down on a rolling tray and pushed it over next to Cass. She looked around. "You still all right sitting in the chair or do you want to get back in bed?"

"I'll sit here a little longer. If I need to, Shelby can help me get back in bed."

"Okay," Jess glanced at Shelby. "If you need some help moving her, make sure you come get me. It's no big deal and I would rather come help than have her fall."

"I'll call if I need help, I promise." Shelby punctuated the statement with a brief salute.

Jess laughed at the gesture, returning the salute and left them alone again.

Shelby helped Cass open up one of the packets of crackers. She still had the IV in her one hand and had trouble using her fingers to open the plastic packaging.

Cass picked up the cup of juice and sipped at the straw sticking out of the lid.

"Mmmm, apple juice," Cass said.

"I bet that tastes good," Shelby said. "Here, try some peanut butter crackers. Eat slowly, though. You don't want to make yourself sick. You haven't had anything real to eat for more than a day."

Cass nodded and took a bite and savored the sweet and salty taste of the crackers.

"Did the doctor say anything about when you could go home?" Shelby asked.

"I told her I have to be home and back to university by Tuesday."

"Isn't that awfully soon?"

"I can't afford to stay here, Shelby. If my parents find out what happened, they'll want to come see me. There'll be no way for me to hide all of this. I have to wait until my hair grows back enough to cover up the implants on the side of my face."

"I know why you want to hide it, Cass. You don't have to, though."

"You don't understand, Shel. Just take my word for it. I have to make sure I get back before they realize anything happened or it'll be bad."

"All right, you're the boss."

Shelby didn't look convinced, but Cass had at least planted the suggestion that they were all going home together as planned on Monday afternoon.

She knew she still had to convince the doctor to discharge her and find a way to hide any financial charges from the hospital from her family. Some of that would be covered under her insurance program through the university, but there would be additional charges that wouldn't be covered.

She could put some of that on her own expense chip, but the rest would have to be paid out later. She had to make sure the bill came to her and was not sent accidentally to her parents.

Cass and Shelby sat together in silence while Cass finished eating the crackers and drank the rest of the juice. It all tasted good and satisfied her hunger pangs. Soon after she finished, Cass felt herself drifting off to sleep again.

After the second time Cass nodded off while Shelby was talking to her, Shelby stood up.

"All right, let's get you back in bed. You're ready to go back to sleep again. The nurses have all said you need to get your rest. That's especially true if you intend to go home tomorrow. Don't worry, I'll stay here with you while you sleep."

Cass nodded. She felt a little bit better about things now that Shelby was here with her. She'd also had a chance to think and adjust to it all. She was still worried, but with Shelby beside her, Cass felt like she could conquer anything.

That was one thing Shelby always offered her. Her girlfriend had a tremendous sense of self-confidence and always believed there was a way out of any situation. Her mood when she got like that was infectious. Cass hoped it was enough to help her make it through the next few weeks.

Chapter 12

A WEEK LATER, Cass returned to her room after her last class of the day and sat down on her bed. Her head ached and she needed to take something for it. The headaches she got when she overdid things had gotten a little better each day since her return.

The doctors back on the island had warned her against pushing herself too quickly. Cass ignored their concerns. She couldn't afford to miss any school and took special care to make sure her grades didn't suffer, leaving her parents wondering why.

Keeping her parents in the dark about her injuries had been tricky. She'd managed to avoid her parents' two video calls when she got back the first day. That gave Cass and Shelby time the next day to go out into the city and find a wig matching her own hair color.

It took them several stops to find what they were looking for. In the end, they found one that was almost perfect. The cut was a little different and shorter than her own style, but Cass was able to make it fit and the hair hung down on the right side just enough to hide the implant on her cheek when she sat in front of her tablet's camera.

The wig, and some extra make up to cover her still healing bruises, managed to get Cass through the next couple of face-chats with her parents. Aside from her mother commenting on her new haircut, she was able to keep them from noticing anything else was different.

Cass flopped down across her bed and closed her eyes. There were some things about her new implants she was still getting used to. Thankfully, Shelby had been a big help with that.

The first time she enabled the cybernetics circuits in her new cerebral core to reach out to the Mantle, Cass had a full-blown panic attack. The whole concept frightened her to her core.

Shelby helped her get through it, though. It was overwhelming nonetheless. The sheer bulk of information that flooded into Cassie's consciousness was both amazing and daunting. In an instant, Cass knew where other connected devices and robots were in relation to herself. She could place herself on any map down to where she stood in her dorm room. It was more accurate than any old-school GPS System could be.

The big trick for her after first connecting was trying to filter through all the information. Shelby assured her it would be easier as time went by and eventually become automatic, in the same way her human brain normally filtered the information coming in from her eyes and ears.

Speaking of her eyes and ears, Cass took a second to save the lecture recordings from the day's classes. One of the benefits of her implants was she could do local recording of anything she came into contact with. Her system automatically recorded both audio and video to short-term memory systems. She could then gather specific memories from there before it was purged at the end of the day for long-term storage.

She was still getting used to using the recordings but the whole process made it much easier to study than ever before. She no longer needed to take lecture notes by stylus on her tablet. She had everything she needed right in her mind all the time. She could recall it at a moment's notice.

She also had access to a system of apps that enabled her to create text transcriptions of anything she overheard. She could search those transcriptions whenever she needed to check back on something. It made finding information from a professor's lecture simple.

The door creaked as Shelby walked into the room. Cass opened her eyes and smiled.

"Hey," Shelby said. "You look tired. How was class today? Are you feeling all right?"

"It was better. I have a headache just like I've had every day, but it's not as bad this time. That seems to be getting better at least. The doctor told me it would happen that way so I guess I'm on the mend."

"I'm glad to hear that." Shelby sat down on the bed and put her arm around Cass, pulling her close. "I still wish you'd taken them up on the opportunity to go to the rehab place near campus. The docs and nurses there could have made your transition a lot easier. I'm sure the school would have allowed you to make up the work and turn things in late."

Cass shook her head. "I told you, that cost wasn't covered under the University health system. I can't afford to have a charge for a place like that show up on my account. My parents will notice it right away and want to know why I was there."

Shelby fell silent and didn't say anything for a while. Cass knew why. Shelby still didn't believe her parents would really reject her simply because of a medically-necessary implant. Cass was tired of trying to explain it to her. She didn't know them the way Cass did.

"Let's get something to eat," Cass suggested. "My headaches are better after I eat something."

"Sounds like a plan," Shelby said. "Where do you want to go? The cafeteria doesn't open for another half hour."

"Why don't we go to the Special Grind?"

The Special Grind had become their favorite coffeehouse when they ate off-campus. It wasn't too far from their dormitory and had become a hang out for many of the students in the residence halls nearby. It not only served coffee and other beverages, they also had sandwiches and other light fare.

"That sounds like a great idea," Shelby said. "We can use it as an opportunity for you to practice using your access point to place an order."

"I don't know about that. I am really not comfortable using my implant for things like that."

Shelby smiled. "Cass, you have to get over this fear that somehow the Mantle, the net, or somebody's robot brain is going to take over your mind. Just because you're accessing information or sending messages using your implant doesn't mean you're risking anything. It doesn't work that way, no matter what your parents told you growing up."

Cass shrugged. Shelby didn't understand how hard it was to rid herself of years of indoctrination into the Sapiens dogma. Cass never had any contact with the Mantle or any artificial intelligence growing up. The computers they used were considered "dumb" and useful for only the most basic tasks. Because of that, Cass had no frame of reference. She only knew what she was told. It made her more than a little wary of her new capabilities.

"You'd be proud of me. I recorded all my lectures today and even had them transcribed and indexed for keywords without freaking out once."

"That's awesome, Cass. See and nothing hijacked your brain. You're still you."

"Yeah, I guess so."

"That's what I'm trying to tell you," Shelby said. "There's not some insidious mechanical robot force trying to take over humanity. The Mantle is only an artificial intelligence system to help us live more efficient lives. Because of your implants, you have the unique ability to be tied into it more directly than most people are."

"Yeah, I know all that. It just takes some getting used to. Give me some time, Shel. I need to work up to it slowly."

"That's exactly why we're going to let you do the ordering on our way to Special Grind. Come on, let's go. We can go ahead and pull up the menu now so you can think about what you want to eat and drink on the way there. I'll do it at the same time so we can walk through the process together."

Cass knew Shelby wasn't going to take no for an answer. That was part of the reason why Cass relied on her so much. Her girlfriend kept pushing her to use her new systems more and more, despite her objections and fears.

So far, it seemed to be working. At least, it was working according to what Shelby told her to expect. This would be the first time she used it to send an open system message to another connected entity. In this case, she would contact the AI running Special Grind's ordering and payment system.

Cass grabbed her key card out of habit as they left. She didn't need it anymore to swipe herself back into the building but it felt good to have it with her anyway. Her implant systems automatically communicated with the campus system once it identified her upon her return. That connection now let her in through any locked door with community access on campus. It included specific access to her dorm room.

Cass had to admit it was convenient when her hands were full of stuff from the local convenience store or when carrying laundry back up from the basement.

She picked up her pace to catch up to Shelby a few steps ahead of her. As they walked towards the cafe, Shelby reached out to Cass via her own implant, sending her the connection address to make their order.

The menu appeared in Cass's mind as both a text and visual message. She scrolled through the menu and saw the image of the panini special of the day. Along with the image was a text description beneath it. Cass selected that, adding it to their order. She also saw the frozen coffee drink Shelby always ordered. Cass added that to their order, too.

"I got it, Shel. Is that everything?" Cass asked.

"That's it. See, that wasn't so hard, was it?"

"No. But you're still not going to tell me that it's as easy as this all the time. What about when the system doesn't work as intended? Anything electronic or mechanical breaks down eventually. Then what do I do?"

"The nano bots the doctors installed in your body, along with the implant's self-repair systems will take care of most of that. For any major repair or damage from an injury or fall, your own system diagnostics will notice it well before you have any major issue. You just go and have a cybernetics specialist look in on it and make any necessary adjustments. It's that simple."

"I don't want to go into the shop every time my brain isn't working the way it's programmed to."

"Stop thinking about it that way, Cass. You're still you. Your organic brain is still there, it's just interfacing with something new. That's all it is. Consider it a supplement to add functionality to what you already have."

Shelby reached out to hold Cass's hand as they continued down the street. She didn't say anything else to Cass or offer more advice. She just gave her hand a gentle squeeze and held it as they walked together to the coffee shop.

Cass realized as long as she had Shelby with her here on campus, she was much more confident in her ability to deal with the changes in her life. It worried her, though. She didn't know what she'd end up doing when the semester was over and she had to return home.

Chapter 13

CASS WOKE up the next morning to an incoming text message from her father. It was still strange to her to receive one directly via her connection to the Mantle over her implant. The words seemed to hover in front of her via the neural input from her right eye. She stared at them, marveling for brief second at how much her life had changed. Then she remembered who the message was from.

Cass, I want to connect with you later. Let me know when you can face chat this afternoon.

Cass grimaced. She'd deceived her parents on two different occasions so far. She wasn't exactly worried about talking with her father again this afternoon, but it still made her anxious. He probably only wanted to see how she did on the test in her psych class this week.

She rolled over to hug Shelby where she lay curled up against her side. Shelby murmured something in her sleep and threw her left arm across Cass's waist.

Cass glanced down and saw the smooth contour of Shelby's cybernetic forearm and hand. She no longer recoiled from touching it. She didn't even notice when Shelby reached out to her with that arm anymore. She accepted her girlfriend's differences without question or apprehension. It was a big step for them and it helped her to accept the things that had changed for herself, too.

Sliding out from under Shelby's arm, Cass got out of bed and left to use the bathroom down the hall from their room. No one was up yet this early on a Saturday and she had the bathroom to herself.

Cass made a point to get up early to be alone. The implant still made her self-conscious. Several people on her floor noticed it when she got back from the trip and commented on it. Most of them thought it was a spur of the moment decision she'd made in a drunken stupor on fall break.

Eventually, word got around to most of them that it had involved a medical emergency. That didn't stop them from staring at her face as she walked by.

As Cass washed her hands, she looked up into the mirror, catching her profile in the reflection. She didn't look that different from before, at least she didn't think so. The implant was there, though, no matter how much she wished it was gone.

The hair had started to grow back on that side where the surgeons had shaved it. The follicle stimulator the doctors gave her helped with that. Soon, it would be long enough to reach down to her shoulders on that side as it had been before the accident.

Cass leaned forward until she was only a few inches away from the mirror. She stared at the cybernetic right eye gazing back as her. Cass made an adjustment with her mind. The eye began to glow with a blue backlight just barely visible in the well-lit bathroom.

She didn't know why that particular option made her smile. It was a purely aesthetic enhancement. It served no function other than to draw attention to the cybernetic eye.

Cass turned off the blue glow and the eye faded to normal. The surgeons did a good job matching up the color to her real eye.

After splashing water on her face and drying off, Cass headed back to the room. Shelby had an outing of some sort planned for them later. She'd told Cass it was a surprise, refusing to tell her anything else about it. Cass was excited to see what it was.

Shelby rolled over in bed and smiled at her as she came back to the room. "Hey, you're up early."

"I got a text from my dad. He wants to talk to me later today. How long are we going to be at this thing you have planned?"

"It won't be long. We should be back a little after lunch time. Will that be all right?"

"It should be. He said he wanted to talk this afternoon. I'll send him a message telling him to check in with me around three o'clock."

"That should be perfect," Shelby said.

"Are you hungry?" Cass asked. "I'm feeling like my stomach is going to shrink to nothing if I don't get something to eat soon. I swear all I do is eat all the time."

"You'll get used to it, I promise," Shelby said with a laugh.

Shelby referred to the fact that Cass's new cybernetics required additional energy to operate. The need for more blood sugar to power the implants increased her caloric needs by a significant amount.

Cass never had to watch what she ate before the injury, but she'd never been one to eat a lot of food in one sitting either. Now she was eating amounts that astounded her. She felt like the electronic interface chewed up those calories as fast as she could eat them. Because of that, Cass had lost weight since the accident despite her attempt to eat more.

She tossed Shelby a sweatshirt from the laundry basket. "Why don't you get up and get some clothes on. We can head over to the cafeteria together. It opens in a few minutes."

Shelby nodded and sat up, swinging her legs over the side of the bed and sitting for a moment as she rubbed her eyes.

Cass waited while she pulled on the sweatshirt and a pair of shorts and headed down the hall to the bathroom. Shelby came back and slipped on some sweatpants and announced she was ready to go.

"I hope they have the waffle station open this morning," Cass said. "I plan on eating four or five of them."

"Don't worry, hon," Shelby assured her with a chuckle. "They'll have something for you to eat. I promise."

All through breakfast, Cass tried to get Shelby to tell her what they were doing later that morning.

Shelby smiled each time and said, "You'll just have to wait. I promise you it'll be something that will open your eyes in a way you haven't had before. This is going to be an important step for you, sweetie."

Cass considered the cryptic words from her girlfriend. Shelby loved surprises. This was just another one of her attempts at catching Cass off-guard. Because of that, she didn't want to give Shelby the satisfaction of seeing her squirm.

Even so, Cass bubbled with anticipation beneath the surface as they finished breakfast and headed back to the dorm. "If we're going out, I should know what to wear."

"I would wear something warm. It's going to be chilly out today," Shelby said. "We'll be walking outside at least part of the time and where we're going doesn't have heat, so you'll want to be comfortable."

Cass thought maybe they were headed to the city park. There was often a festival or fair happening on weekends. She resisted the urge to access her connection to the Mantle for a listing of events going on in the city. Despite the way she felt, Cass didn't like to spoil surprises. She also still cringed almost every time she had to access the Mantle for something.

Back in the room, Cass pulled on a clean pair of leggings instead of the sweatpants she'd worn to breakfast. She also got out a wool sweater and her winter vest. That should keep her warm wherever they were going but not overheat her if they ended up indoors for a while at some point.

"Do I need a hat or anything?" Cass asked. She had picked up her wig and stood in front of the mirror to put it on. If she didn't have to wear it and could get away with merely a hat she'd prefer that.

"No, it's not going to be super cold today just a little chilly and windy. You don't have to wear that thing, either. Leave the wig here. I like you just the way you are and honestly the way your hair is partially shaved back on that side is kind of hot."

Cass's hand drifted up to the right side of her head. She pulled it back down again, self-conscious of her injury and implant. She worried about people staring at her.

"I'll wear it if it's all right with you," Cass said. She pulled on the wig and stared into the mirror as she shifted it into place. She brushed a few stray strands of hair into place and smiled. She looked a lot more like herself again.

"Are you ready?" Shelby asked. She didn't hide her disappointment with the wig.

Cass ignored the response and changed the subject. "Are you going to tell me where we're going now?"

"You'll see," Shelby said with a laugh. She led Cass out of the dorm. An auto cab already waited for them at the curb. Most people didn't own personal vehicles anymore. They trusted the driverless cars when they needed safe transportation around the city.

Her parents, of course, didn't trust anything that used the Mantle to navigate so they and other Sapiens families still used old-fashioned vehicles configured for manual operation.

Cass climbed in the back seat with Shelby and sat back while the car pulled away from the curb and drove downtown. The city had many different neighborhoods. The University sat in one of the more affluent areas. Cass covered her surprise as the car turned into one of the nearby neighborhoods her father had warned her about when she first arrived.

The car pulled over to the curb and a chime sounded, signaling they had reached their destination. The crowd of people on the sidewalks outside the car looked like variations on a melding between people and robots. There were all sorts of enhancements visible.

A man with what looked like silver skin over his entire body passed by her car window walking an android dog. Next to him walked a woman with shimmering strands of foil hanging down from her head like hair. It sparkled with rainbow hues in the bright sunlight overhead.

Every single person on the street had at least one major cyber body enhancement. Most were more extreme than just v-tats, though there were quite a few of those in evidence, too.

"Shelby, what are we doing here? Is this neighborhood safe?"

"It's perfectly safe, Cass. These people may not look like what you're used to, but they aren't criminals or gang-bangers. Come on out. I want to show you something. There's a whole world waiting out there for you."

Shelby climbed out and waited on the curb. Cass slid across the seat and got out beside her. The auto cab drove away leaving them on the curb in the strange neighborhood.

Cass moved closer to Shelby and her hand drifted down to grip her girlfriend's, their fingers interlacing.

"Cass, relax. It's going to be fine. Nobody here's going to hurt you."

"If you say so," Cass said. She couldn't stop herself from staring as a woman walked by on metal stilts in place of legs. Cass hoped she had lost her legs in an accident. Who cut off their legs like that on purpose?

"Come on," Shelby said, pulling Cass's attention back to her. "Follow me."

Cass didn't let go of Shelby's hand, staying by her side as she led the two of them to an alley between two buildings.

Cass held back from the shadowy side street. "Shelby, are you sure?"

"Trust me. Prepare to be amazed."

Shelby stopped halfway down the alley in front of a door in the side of one of the buildings. She pulled open the door, revealing a metal staircase leading down.

The only small comfort for Cass was the stairwell was well-lit. It shouldn't have mattered. After all, she could see in near total darkness now. Old habits kept her watching for trouble, though.

Shelby tugged at Cass's hand and together they started down the steps. The door closed behind them with a clang.

Their steps echoed as they descended. After the first two flights, the sound of high-energy dance music drifted up to her ears from below. It sounded like there was a party of some sort going on down there.

The stairs turned through several more landings before reaching the bottom. When they stepped out of the stairwell, Cass stood with her mouth open, staring at the mob of people filling the underground parking garage in front of her.

Stretched out before her was a large underground garage area. There were tables and display stalls set up all along the perimeter and in rows down each section of the concrete floor. Each of the tables or stalls had items or services for display and sale.

It only took a few seconds for Cass to realize all the stalls had something to do with cyber-enhancement or personal image for a cyber-human. Some of the vendors sold things as simple as pierced earrings with tiny LED projectors inside them. Others offered instant v-tat installation for those that were willing to sit for the procedure. She saw several people lined up next to those tables. They were popular it seemed.

"So, what do you think?" Shelby asked.

"I don't know what to think," Cass replied. "What is this place?"

"This is the Bizarre. This is where the city's cyber-human population comes to show off their look, add to their style, and talk about what they want to have done next."

"Shel, I don't want to get anything done," Cass said. "You know that, right?"

"No one's going to do anything you don't want, Cassie. I thought it was important for you to see the new world open to you now. These people are all just like you."

Cass knew Shelby meant well. Despite the fact several people in their dorm had v-tats and other similar minor enhancements, very few students had any sort of major add-ons like Shelby and herself.

Cass knew the population of truly enhanced cyber-human persons in the country as a whole was less than a half percent. She had that information from her father's statistics. He talked about them all the time. Cass knew she was in a very small minority of people, but that didn't automatically make her one of them in her mind.

In an effort to be polite and to cover her uneasiness, Cass forced a smile. "I guess it wouldn't hurt to look around a little."

"That's what I thought you'd say. Come on, I want to show you around. My brother's supposed to be here somewhere and I want to introduce you to him."

Cass smiled genuinely at that. She'd wanted to meet Shelby's brother for a while. She talked about him all the time. He was an activist in the cyber-human community, advocating for equal rights and protections for all.

She followed Shelby around the room, stopping occasionally to check out an item here and there at one of the stalls. Her eyes drifted again and again to the v-tat studios around the room. Each of them were well attended and had a line of at least two or three people waiting their turn.

Shelby spotted Cass checking out a woman getting a new v-tat installed across her upper back. "Are you thinking about getting one?" Shelby asked, running her hand up Cass's back.

"No, I was just checking them out."

"You and I could get one together." Shelby squeezed Cass's hand as she said it. Cass surprised herself when she nodded and said, "That might be nice."

"Really?" Shelby couldn't hide her surprise. "Um, I think it might be fun to get something like a tropical palm tree waving in the breeze or something like that."

"Why something like that?"

"A lot of people get things that signify the underlying reason for getting their enhancements. It's sort of a rite of passage. For you and I, it could signal our trip to the islands and what happened to you there."

"I don't think I want to commemorate that occasion, Shel. I would do anything to forget it ever happened."

Shelby started to say something and stopped.

Cass waited, trying to calm herself before saying anything else.

Eventually, Shelby found her voice. "I'm sorry, Cass. Forget I said anything. Come on. Let's find Eric. He's excited to meet you."

Chapter 14

CASS AND SHELBY continued browsing around the Bizarre while Shelby tried to locate her brother. They found him standing in front of a booth displaying several custom options for cybernetic hands.

Some of the options looked almost human with supple pink or brown skin. Others looked more alien in nature. Cass thought some of the options to be downright frightening and creepy.

Scanning the collection of hands and arms lying out on the table as they approached distracted Cass. She didn't see Shelby's reaction to the young man standing and chatting with the vendor. Her girlfriend ran up behind him and jumped on his back. She flung her arms around his shoulders and her legs around his waist.

"Eric!"

Though Shelby's apparent assault on a stranger shocked Cass at first, the move didn't surprise Shelby's brother at all. He reached down and grabbed Shelby's legs under her knees to hold her in place and turned around towards Cass, laughing along with Shelby.

Eric was about six feet tall, which put him just a few inches taller than his sister. His head was shaved, showing off a one-inch wide metal bar running from the back of his head, across the top, and ending just above his eyes. Instead of eyebrows, another, thinner metal bar stretched across just above his eyes. It mounted a mirrored glass visor in front of his eyes. The visor had a curved cut out for his nose and fit up against the skin of his face all the way around.

Cass couldn't see his eyes, instead the visor projected a single holographic eye, like that of a cyclops, in the middle of the screen. The eye rotated in place as if looking around. When it locked onto Cass, seeming to meet her gaze, she looked away.

"Hey, sis, how the heck are you?"

"Did I surprise you?" Shelby asked.

"You can't surprise me, kid. You haven't been able to sneak up on me in a long time."

A brief flash of disappointment spread across Shelby's face. It disappeared as fast as it arrived, replaced by a huge grin. She let go with her arms and legs, sliding back to the floor.

Eric smiled at Cass and pointed to her. "Is this who I think it is?"

Moving around in front of her brother, Shelby gestured to Cass. "Eric, this is Cass."

Eric stepped forward, surprising Cass by pulling her into an embrace. "It is so nice to meet you finally, Cass. You're making my sister very happy. She never stops talking about you."

"I feel the same way about you," Cass replied as Eric let go of her and stepped back.

Eric smiled and gestured around at the underground market-place. "So, what do you think? Shelby told me this is your first time to a cyber-friendly swap-meet. It must be a lot to take in to the uninitiated."

"It is pretty different from what I expected," Cass said. "Of course, I never even knew places like this existed until today. Everyone is so friendly. I expected it to be sort of..."

"What? Dangerous maybe?" Eric laughed. "That's what a lot of the mainstreamers would have people think about us. They don't understand why we go to all the trouble to express ourselves this way. Some of the extreme radicals think we're trying to create some sort of master race of cyber people. That's not the case at all."

Cass nodded and looked around at the surrounding booths in this part of the underground marketplace. Across the aisle, a woman lay back, reclined in an old-style dentist's chair. Cass gasped when she realized the woman had just had a new implant placed in her head. A metal skull cap covering the crown of her shaved head sat in place while another woman bent over her. The second woman stretched the skin up over the metal margins of the cap. She used a dermal regenerator to adhere the skin to the edges of the circular cap, affixing the glowing red beam from the regenerator's wand all the way around the margins until there was no gap between the skin and the edge of the device.

Shelby came over and stood next to Cass, watching the procedure while reaching down to hold her hand. "Cass is still pretty new to all this. I think it's a bit of a shock to her."

"Shelby," Cass said, resisting the urge to point at what was essentially surgery taking place just a few yards away in this dirty underground parking garage. "Why aren't they getting that done in a hospital? It can't be safe to do it here. It isn't sanitary."

Eric stepped up beside them and said, "You were the exception and not the norm when you got your implant, Cass. Most people like us can't afford to get our add-ons in a hospital setting. We have to settle for doing it in places like this. It's not as bad as it looks. That woman working on her will inject a supply of nano bots into the patient. That'll not only complete the neural connections, it'll also fight off most infections that may arise."

Cass glanced at Shelby. "Did you get your arm attached in a place like this? And your cerebral implant?"

Shelby nodded. "As Eric said, not everyone has the funds to get a real doctor to do this kind of work. Even those who do tend to be discreet. The wealthy cover up their more advanced and compact high-end implants, so no one knows they have them. The rest of us have to settle for older, aftermarket and custom gear."

"That's hardly fair," Cass said.

Shelby nodded. "The world's not exactly fair. The rest of us have to make do with what we have available to us." She turned to her brother. "See, Eric, I told you she has a lot of misinformation about us to overcome."

He shook his head, although he smiled. "I can't believe you're a

Sapiens member and your dad works for Sterling Noble. That bastard wants to put all of us into cages."

"No, he doesn't want that at all," Cass replied. She answered out of reflex, defending her father and the man she knew as the leader of the Sapiens movement. "It's about keeping the rest of us safe from those who would exploit the humans without enhancements."

"The rest of us?" Eric asked. "Have you read any of his most recent speeches?" His mood darkened. Cass could tell because the screen of his visor changed to dark swirling clouds with occasional lightning flashing across it. It was similar to the way Shelby's v-tats shifted with her emotions.

"I've met him and he's not a horrible person. He just wants people to remain people and not become machines under control of someone or something else."

"But you're a…" Eric started to respond.

Shelby put up her hand and interrupted them. "Hey, you two, let's not have a fight. I want you two to get along. Cass is still adjusting to some things about herself and our community. She doesn't really understand who we are and what we stand for."

After a few seconds, the visor across Eric's eyes shifted once again, returning to the single eye floating in a grey background.

He smiled. "You're right, sis. I'm sorry, Cass. I get upset about people wanting to lock me up just because I'm different. I thought you would feel the same way now that you have your own implants to contend with. How are your parents reacting to your upgrades?"

Cass didn't think of them as upgrades, though she knew that's what people in counter-culture cyber-human circles considered them. She stammered out the beginning of a reply but Shelby stopped her.

"She hasn't told her parents yet, Eric. She's afraid of how they'll react to what was done after the accident."

Eric nodded. The cyclops eye on the visor had a single tear form in the corner and drop away. He reached out his hand, placing it on Cass's shoulder. "It sucks when your family doesn't accept who you are. In this community, it's different. If you accept us, we accept you, no matter how you look or who you are. We're all about a live and let live approach to life. We celebrate people's differences."

Cass offered a half-smile at Eric's attempt to reassure her. It all still overwhelmed her. Directly behind Eric, a guy in his twenties scooted by so fast, she thought he was riding a skateboard. As he came around the corner into full view, she realized he'd added wheels to his ankles in place of his feet. She stared as he lost his balance and careened into one of the tables, falling down and knocking a bunch of the items for sale to the floor.

The whole absurd scene hit her and she began to laugh in spite of herself.

Eric and Shelby turned around to see what she was looking at and the two began laughing along with her. The owner of the booth stood over him shouting about the scattered merchandise.

The guy on the ground tried to help and gather the fallen items into his hands and put them back on the table. The problem was he couldn't get back to his feet. The wheels kept slipping out from under him.

Eric smiled and gestured towards the hapless fellow. "Let's go give them a hand, Shelby. He's obviously new to his wheels."

Eric and Shelby went over and helped the guy up, holding him under his arms and standing beside him until he got his wheeled feet back under him. Cass followed them over and bent down to help the booth's owner pick up the rest of the scattered merchandise. It looked like most of it was some sort of circuit board chipset inside a clear acrylic box.

"Thanks," the wheelie guy said to Shelby and Eric while they steadied him from either side. "I don't know what I was thinking when I ordered these. I figured I'd be able to use them to handle my delivery jobs a lot faster than riding my bicycle the way I used to."

"You probably just need to adjust to it first," Eric said. "With a little practice, I'll bet you'll be super fast and zipping around the city like you were born with wheels."

"I hope you're right. I spent a lot of money getting these. Robot delivery services are faster than I am. I hoped this would help me compete."

"I think it's super rad," Shelby added. "I'll bet it cost you a bunch, though. Didn't they come with gyro stabilizing systems and upgrades for your cortical implant?"

The guy nodded and tapped a small metal plate behind his ear. "I'm still getting used to the new system. I guess I should've taken the guy's advice and walked with a cane or something for the next few days. I didn't think it would be necessary, but now I'm beginning to reconsider."

Eric looked around. "Is he here? Maybe we can help you get back to his booth and he can give you that cane he offered."

"That would be super nice. He's over a few rows and towards the far side."

Cass put the last of the acrylic circuit boxes on the vendor's table. The man behind the table grumbled a thank you to her. She nodded and turned to follow the others as they helped wheelie guy back down the aisle.

With Shelby and Eric on either side of him and Cass trailing behind, the guy rolled through the Bizarre and down the next row over until he stopped in front of a larger booth with a medical exam chair set behind a series of display tables. The gentleman behind the counter was adding something to the end of a woman's arm when they rolled up.

The vendor at the table turned around, magnifier glasses flipping up automatically as he looked up from his work. He smiled. "I knew you'd be back. I also figured you'd need help getting here. Give me a minute to finish this up and I'll get that cane for you."

The man with the wheeled feet nodded and reached out to steady himself on the end of the table. Eric and Shelby let go of his arms and stepped back.

"Thank you both," the man said. "I really appreciate your help."

"Hey, we've got to stick together," Eric said. "After all, it's us against them."

Cass saw the man smile. Eric's choice of words concerned her. How was his adversarial position any different from what he complained about in Sterling Noble and the Sapiens movement? Eric sounded almost militant with comments like that.

Her father once told her there were underground groups ready to carry out terrorist attacks on unsuspecting pure humans. Could Eric be part of one of those cells?

Cass filed her questions about Eric and his activities away as he and Shelby rejoined her. She decided to push her doubts away and focus on having a good time with Shelby.

The three of them walked down the row, checking out various items and enhancements as they went. Shelby never stopped smiling as she talked with Eric. She was happier than Cass had ever seen before aside from when the two of them were together.

Cass knew Shelby adored her brother and it showed. He was her only family still living close to her here at school. Their parents had sold their home and moved up to Boston to live with her sick grandmother over the summer.

"Cass, I'm so glad you got to come and meet Eric."

"Yeah, Cass," Eric said. "It's good to finally meet the girl who's stolen my sister's heart. I hope we can be friends despite the way my political views cloud my judgment sometimes. I have to remember it's about education and not fighting back. Forgive me?"

"Of course, and, yes, it would be nice to be friends," Cass replied.

"Awesome. I'm glad."

"What should we do next, bro?" Shelby asked.

"I can hang with you gals a little bit longer," Eric said. "I do need to meet with some people later. I just got word of a Sapiens rally coming to the city sometime soon. My contact at City Hall doesn't know when it is yet, but we want to be ready to stage a counter-protest when it happens. We have to show how we stand up to their kind of hate and bigotry."

"The Sapiens are coming here?" Shelby asked. She shot a glance at Cass.

Cass shook her head. This was the first she'd heard of it. Her father hadn't said anything about it when she talked with her parents earlier in the week. It worried her. If there was a rally of some sort planned, her dad would probably want her to be involved with it in some way. She knew she couldn't do that. Not now, not ever.

"Sorry, Shel. I haven't heard anything about anything like that," Cass said.

"All we have is a rumor," Eric said. "I have friends who have a few contacts within the Sapiens organization, but they're not very highly placed. Sometimes they give us information that isn't accurate."

"You have spies in the Sapiens movement?" Cass asked, surprised.

"We have to do what we have to do," Eric said. "There's a civil war on the horizon. If people don't start learning to accept every-one's differences, it's going to happen."

The words civil war scared Cass. She remembered hearing her father and mother talk in much the same way. If both sides thought the outcome was inevitable, what would stop an open conflict?

She felt like she was getting pulled in multiple directions. She'd grown up believing everything her father said was true. Now, Eric's words conflicted with things her father said while still having a similar fatalistic vision of the future.

Shelby tried to change the subject. "Hey, let's go get something to eat. I'm hungry. I'll bet both of you are, too."

Cass got the hint and dropped it.

"I think that would be an awesome idea," Eric said. "Has Cass ever been to O'Malley's?"

"No," Cass said. "What's O'Malley's?"

"Only the best diner in the whole city," Eric replied. "Come on, let's leave and head down there. It's only a few blocks away. You're going to love their burgers. They are literally the best in the world."

Cass nodded. She was hungry again. She and Shelby followed Eric as the three of them left the underground cyber-market to return to the city above.

As they walked along, Cass tried to sort out the feelings swirling through her brain. She wanted to like Shelby's brother. He was important to her and that made him important to Cass, too. His views were more radical than she'd expected, though.

She also wanted to believe the things Shelby told her as she learned about the cyber-human world. She was part of that world now whether she wanted it or not.

<hr>

Chapter 15

<hr>

DESPITE THE CONCERNS swirling through her mind, Cass enjoyed their lunch at O'Malley's diner. The three of them sat and chatted about Shelby's youth and family life for more than an hour.

Eric's personality was infectious. It was hard not to like him. He was funny and exciting to talk to. He was passionate about ensuring that cyber-humans received the rights he felt they deserved, but didn't talk about a violent response. She realized he would stand up for himself but do it peacefully. Cass knew what her father would say about Eric, though.

As she thought about it, she remembered she'd promised her father to be available for a face chat later that day. She checked the time. It was nearly two-thirty in the afternoon. Their time together had distracted her. She and Shelby would have to hurry to get back to the dorm.

In her rush to figure out how long it would take her to get back to the university, Cass's implant automatically connected to the Mantle. She didn't realize she was accessing it until she'd checked the map and gotten the ETA from it.

Cass disconnected as soon as she realized what had happened. Her implant did that more and more as her brain integrated with it and began to share the processing of information. The connection came without thought now. It made Cass wonder if that was a sign. Was she coming under the influence of the Mantle's global AI?

"Shelby," Cass said. "We need to be going. My father is expecting me to chat with him and I'd like to do it in private."

Eric's expression changed as she mentioned her father. Cass didn't miss the frown that briefly passed across his face. Even the visor's background changed to a deep red for an instant before returning to neutral gray again.

Eric didn't say anything, though. His expression returned to the easy-going smile he had when she first met him.

For some reason, that made her like him even more. He didn't seem to hold her family against her. Sure, her father was a Sapiens leader, but that didn't mean she was lumped in with him automatically. Cass wasn't sure she'd have been as open if their roles were reversed.

Shelby slid out of the booth and stood to make room for Cass to get up, too. "I'll call us an auto cab."

Cass nodded and turned back to Eric. "It was nice to meet you. I hope we get the chance to see each other again sometime soon. I want you to tell me more stories about Shelby when she was little."

Eric laughed. "I will definitely do that. There are quite a few I'd love to share with you."

"That's enough of that," Shelby said. "I don't need you embarrassing me anymore in front of my girlfriend. Remember, turnabout is fair play, brother mine."

Eric held up a hand in surrender. "Fair enough, sis. You two have a great day. I'll cover lunch. Be careful heading back across town."

Shelby and Cass headed outside the diner to wait for the auto cab. It didn't take long to show up and they hopped in the back. Soon, they were heading back towards the university.

Cass got back just in time to race into the dorm room and grab her tablet. She fired up the regular net connection she used with her dad. If the tablet wasn't so dumb, Cass could have used her own

Mantle connection to initiate the link between the tablet's camera and her parents.

Other devices around the campus were set up such that she could talk directly to them through her implant. She didn't even have to use her hands to operate some appliances.

Cass checked her implant's internal clock. It was almost time for her dad to call and he was always punctual.

Cass stood and glanced in the mirror across the room above her dresser to make sure her wig was still in place to cover up the implant. Just to be safe, Cass set the tablet on her desk angled in such a way so that it favored the other side of her face when she sat down.

The connection rang on the table. Cass tapped the accept button and she saw her father's face smiling back from the other side.

"Hi, sweetie," James Armstrong said. "I can't believe it's been so long since we've talked to each other."

"It's only been a week, Dad. You act like it's been forever."

"When you're a parent someday, you'll understand how much you miss your kids when they're not around."

Cass smiled. She missed her parents, too. She couldn't tell them she had her own reasons for avoiding talking to them. Cass jerked her hand back to her lap as she caught herself subconsciously reaching up to touch her implant.

"You said you had some news, Dad. What is it?"

"I thought I'd surprise you, but your mother told me to make sure you knew first."

"Knew what?"

"That I'm coming to the city. I have an event coming up in a few weeks and I'll have some time to spend with you."

"You're coming here?" Cass said, trying to stifle the panic she felt rising within her.

"Yes, there's going to be a big movement rally there with folks coming in from all up and down the coast. I've been asked by Sterling to come and help get things set up in advance."

"A rally for the Sapiens? Here, near the university?"

"Yes," her father said. "Sterling wants us to become more visible and call out the dangerous subs lurking in and around that part of the city when we see them. There's quite a large group of them around there, in case you hadn't noticed. The liberals in the city's government are creating a haven for the freaks. I know you've probably done your best to avoid that type of person, but you should be aware that they're there. We've got some word of a subversive group rising there, too. We figured it was time to show our hand and let them know we're on to them."

Her father's words brought back to mind some of the things Eric had talked about over lunch. Was he one of those subversives her father was talking about?

"Is something wrong, Cass? You have a pained look on your face."

"Oh, no. Sorry, I was distracted by remembering an assignment I have to get done before Monday. I'm glad to hear you're coming. I'll have to thank Mom for making sure you didn't surprise me."

"She suggested that it would be a bad idea if I were to just drop in on you and Shelby. Mom seems to think I could catch you two in a compromising position."

"Dad!" Cass said. Her face flushed at her father's allusion to her relationship with Shelby. How did they know?

James laughed at Cass's reaction, pointing through the screen at her. "Ha, your mother was right. She said she could tell from the way you talked about Shelby that there was something going on between you two. I'm happy you've found someone there at school. I definitely want to meet her this time when I come to visit. I can take the two of you out for a nice dinner."

"I'll see what I can do." Cass was glad she'd asked Shelby to remain in the dorm's common area while she was on the call. "She's super busy and isn't here very often. Her school work keeps her away a lot in the school library and she works part-time, too."

"Well, I hope she's available when I come to town next week."

"Next week? That's so soon." Cass tamped down her rising panic. She'd hoped to have more time to figure out a way to hide her implant in a more permanent way. The wig wouldn't do during a face-to-face meeting.

"Yes, it is, but the planned demonstration is coming up at the end of the month and we wanted to make sure all the proper paperwork for the demonstration and march was filed with the city in plenty of time. That's one of the reasons I'm coming, to smooth things over as Sterling's representative to the city government."

Cass's mind raced as she tried to figure out how she was going to do all the things she needed to do to hide her new life from her father. A week provided her very little time to do so.

James continued without noticing how distracted Cass was. "Anyway, it's good to see your face, Cassie. I can't wait to give you a big hug when I see you next week. I should be getting in sometime Friday morning and once I'm done with my meetings with the city officials and lunch with the mayor, I'll come by the university and pick you and Shelby up for dinner.

"Sounds good, Dad. Thanks for calling."

Her father cut the connection from the other side and Cass let out a long sigh. Shelby's voice caught her by surprise from the other side of the room. "He's right, you know. You can't hide me from your parents forever."

Cass turned around. "How long have you been there?"

"I came in the room about halfway through the call. I didn't want to interrupt you, but I needed to get something from my desk. Don't worry, I made sure to stay out of the video pickup. I know how much hiding me from your parents means to you."

"Shelby don't be like that. You know I have a very good reason not to tell my parents about you, and about me, too."

"Just because you have a reason, doesn't make it a good reason. Your parents are going to find out eventually. You're going to have to face the fact that they may not be the people you think they are."

Cass didn't answer. Shelby was right. She was deathly afraid of her father's reaction to Shelby and her own implants.

Shelby continued. "Eric did a little digging on your dad. I wasn't gonna say anything, but now that we're talking about him, I think maybe you should know."

"Know what?"

"You should know that your father is involved with the Sapiens First wing of the movement."

"Sapiens First is a myth, Shelby. They don't exist. They're just the creation of people who want to paint us as terrorists and bigots."

"So it's us again, is it?" Shelby asked. "It doesn't take much for you to slip back into the party line, does it?"

"Shelby, you're twisting my words. I'm telling you that I would know if there was a secret, underground terrorist movement within my father's political party. I promise you, there's not. All the Sapiens movement is asking for are some simple changes to the law."

"Those changes could make you an outlaw," Shelby pointed out.

"I don't agree with all of their positions anymore, but some of the things they want are very reasonable."

"Cass, the fact that you still believe that makes me want to cry. There are so many things about you I care about and love deeply, but this side of you is so ugly, and it scares me."

Shelby turned and stormed out of the room letting the door close behind her.

Cass's shoulders sank and she bent forward to put her head down on the desk. She couldn't understand how that conversation had gone so wrong so quickly.

Cass knew in some ways Shelby was right about how she was hiding things from her parents. She also knew Shelby was equally wrong in her assumptions about her dad and family and their belief system.

She sat and thought about what she needed to do to make it right with Shelby. Cass needed her help to find someone who could cover up her implant in some way, or at least give her the means to hide it while her father was in town.

Cass got up and headed out of the room after her girlfriend. She had to catch up to Shelby and apologize.

Shelby was already across the street from the dorm, heading towards the center of campus when Cass ran outside.

Cass called out to her as she ran to catch up. "Shelby, stop. Please, I'm sorry."

Shelby turned around. Tears streamed down her cheeks. "What are you sorry about, Cass?"

"I'm sorry about what I said. I know you only want the best for me. I shouldn't have said what I did."

"Whether you like it or not, you're in this just like my brother and me. I know it wasn't your fault but you have to come to grips with who you are now. I can't do that for you. If you're not comfortable being who you are with that implant, you're never going to be able to stand up to your father."

Cass knew deep inside everything Shelby said was true. She had a hard time admitting it to herself aloud, though.

"I need your help, Shelby. My father is coming here and I can't let him see me like this. Now is not the time to confront him about what's happened to me. You have to believe me, he'll be far angrier than you could ever believe or understand."

Shelby paused and didn't say anything for several long seconds. "You know covering it up isn't going to make it go away, right?"

"That's not it. I need more time to get ready to tell them about it."

Shelby sighed. "All right, we'll go tomorrow after our morning classes. There's a guy at the Bizarre that can help us out with this. He used to do cosmetic work for the people who wanted enhancements but didn't want anyone to know they had them. I think he can probably do something that'll work for you, at least temporarily."

"That would be perfect," Cass said.

"It really won't be, Cass. Lying about who you are isn't ever perfect." Shelby reached out and took her hand. "Don't worry, love. I've got your back, even when you're being stubborn."

Cass gave a half smile and pulled Shelby's metal hand up in hers and kissed the warm metal skin. As long as they were together, Cass felt like she could do anything.

Chapter 16

THE NEXT DAY, Cass spotted Shelby waiting for her outside the Liberal Arts building when she got out of class. Cass smiled at her girlfriend sitting on a stone bench in the sunlight outside the building. She was gorgeous and Cass realized all over again how lucky she was to have Shelby in her life.

Shelby stood up as Cass approached. "Ready to go?"

"Yeah. I wanted to thank you again for not staying angry with me over this."

Shelby shrugged. "Staying mad at you is never something I'm going to do, Cass. We're going to get in fights, but I also believe we'll get through them. Come on, I just dialed up an auto cab. It's on its way."

The couple headed across the broad grassy area between the buildings towards the city street nearby. The auto cab waited for them when they got there. Cass opened the door and held it for Shelby, then climbed in behind her. The car pulled away from the curb and headed back downtown towards the Bizarre.

Fifteen minutes later, Cass once again descended the metal stairs to the underground garage. There were fewer people and vendors in the vast open space this time around. Most of the vendors probably had day jobs during the week.

"I hope he's here," Shelby said. "I didn't have any way to get in touch with him so I left a bunch of messages with folks I knew in case they ran into him. I only know about him by reputation."

"You said he does cosmetic work for the wealthy?"

"Yes, he helps those people hide their implant systems in such a way that they can cover up so that no one knows they're there."

It was common knowledge among people in the Sapiens community that more people were covering up implants than ever before. Her father had always told her that the people with implants were secretly converting others to be like them. He believed the Mantle eventually would take over the world and rule humanity if they weren't stopped. He called it an inevitable occurrence.

"I've heard of people getting secret implants," Cass said. "That creates a lot of fear in some people."

"People such as your family?"

"Yes," Cass admitted.

"Most of the enhancements people get are made in such a way they can be serviced from the outside if there's ever a problem. The challenge this provides is that they often make it hard to hide their presence. For those of us who opted for enhancements, we wear that visible evidence as a badge of honor and individuality."

Shelby nodded at a woman nearby who had a set of plastic fairy wings jutting out from between her shoulder blades. They waved slowly behind her in a sort of flapping motion from the point where they connected to an implant in the middle of her back.

"Many of us like to show off our individual preferences and aspirations for something different in ourselves," Shelby continued. "For some among the wealthy, though, they don't wish to be so overt. I guess they consider it crass or something. For those people, they have special miniature implants designed so that they can be entirely internal. It creates a problem because there's still the issue of accessing the implants for repair and upgrades. They accomplish this through specialists in the medical field who help them cover up.

It's super expensive and is one of the things that separates them from others like you and me."

Shelby smiled at Cass. "If you had been injured here in the States, it is likely your insurance would have covered most of the cost of an implant that was entirely internal, if you or your family had wanted to pay the extra fee for it. Then your implant would've been hidden from view except for a small port that could be easily covered up. In the Caribbean, with fewer modern resources, they had to use off-the-shelf modifications to save your life and restore you."

"This guy can help me, though, right? He can make it so that no one knows I have the implant."

Shelby nodded. "I haven't seen his work personally but I know of several people who needed help getting jobs where having an implant would've been a problem. They used what they got from this guy to cover up their enhancements while they're at work. Then they show them off on the weekends they're home."

Shelby pointed across the underground garage. "I think he's at that table over there. That's where Eric told me he usually sets up. Come on. Let's see if it's him."

Cass followed Shelby across the room and down one of the nearly empty rows of vendor stalls until they reached the far wall. There were only a few tables occupied here. One of them had a man with a sort of old-school leather padded exam chair set up behind the table. He had shelves and racks of various bins and what looked like some sort of a 3-D printer set up, too. He stood up as the two women approached. "Hello, ladies. What can I help you two with today?"

"Hi, I'm Shelby and this is my girlfriend, Cass. My brother, Eric Moore, told me to look you up. Cass here has a sort of problem that we hope you can help her with."

"Helping people is what I do." He reached out with one hand to Cass's chin, tilting her head to the left. He nodded. "Are you looking for a permanent cover up or one that you can remove when needed?"

Cass thought about it for a second. She hadn't considered the option of getting a permanent solution to her problem. "What's the difference?"

"Permanent is pricey. It's more than most kids your age can afford but I don't want to make assumptions. I always offer both options."

"I'll go ahead and get one I can take on and off," Cass said. "Is that possible?"

"It shouldn't be a problem," the man said, glancing at the side of Cass's face again. He held out a hand. "I'm Frederick. Some call me the skin doctor, though."

"That's an interesting name," Shelby said.

"It's appropriate though. I am sort of a wizard at this and used to be a doctor before I lost my license."

His revelation startled Cass and she wondered if maybe she should talk to someone else about this.

Frederick noticed her reaction. "The people in the medical community didn't like that I came down here on the weekends and offered my services to people who didn't have access to the funds to get it done in the hospital. They said I was ignoring patient safety but it was really because I was undercutting their profits."

Frederick waved a hand in the air and continued. "I realized I was tired of taking care of the rich and the privileged at the expense of those who really needed my help. Believe me, I'm much happier now."

Cass nodded. His explanation made her feel a little better. "So, what can you do for me?"

"Come on around the table and sit in my chair. Your friend can watch, but she'll need to stay back so that we don't have any problems with infection."

Cass had started around the table but stopped when she heard what he said. "Infection? Are you going to cut into me or something?"

"No, but I do need to fuss with the interface between your skin and the implant a little bit. It's necessary to make the cover-up stay in place. I need to create a sterile field around you. It'll help if your friend stays over there where she can watch but not be close enough to cough or sneeze in this direction."

"Hey, I cover my mouth."

"Not everybody does and it's better if we just be one hundred percent sure just in case one catches you by surprise. Sneezes are like that sometimes," he finished with a wink at Cass.

She smiled. She liked this guy. Continuing around the table, Cass sat in the chair, leaning back and resting her head against the circular headrest.

Frederick pressed the button on the arm of the chair and tilted the back down so that he could get a better look at Cass's face. He sat down on a stool, rolling around on wheels beside the exam chair. Frederick slid up right next to her and leaned over. His hands were warm as he reached out to touch her face. "This is good, clean work. I'm guessing it was a medical implant?"

Cass nodded. "I had an accident recently. This was necessary to help manage my head injury."

"Well, whoever did this is good at what they do. That always makes my job a little easier. All right, let me see what I have here and we'll get you hooked up."

Cass sat in the chair for more than a half hour as Frederick fiddled and tugged on the side of her face. It didn't hurt, though there were a few times where she felt a strange pulling on her cheek. When he was finished, he sat back and looked over at Shelby. "What do you think?"

"Looks pretty good," Shelby said. "If I didn't know the implant was there, I wouldn't be able to tell. It looks a little raised on that side of her face compared to the other, but I guess you have to do that to cover up things."

"Can I see?" Cass asked.

"Of course," Frederick said. He produced a large mirror and held it up in front of Cass. "Let me know what you think."

Cass grabbed the mirror with her right hand and held it up as she turned her face so she could see the right side where the implant was. Her fingers reached out to touch what looked like normal skin there.

She could see what Shelby meant as she examined the patch of synthetic skin. It looked like that side of her face was a little swollen. It wasn't much, but she could tell. Cass marveled at how it felt like normal skin under fingertips. If she pressed down a little bit, she could feel the curved ridge where the implant ran along her cheekbone all the way back to her ear.

"This is wonderful. As long as I wear my hair down on the side, I don't think my family will notice at all. Over time, they'll get used to the slight difference between the two sides."

"That should work, Cass," Shelby said, nodding.

"How much do I owe you, Frederick?"

"That'll be five hundred dollars. You can wire it to me through your credit chip or use your Mantle connection to hook into my account and make a deposit."

It was expensive, but Cass didn't complain about the price. It was actually a little less than she expected it to be, especially given the quality of the work.

"Let me open up my account and I'll send it to you," Cass said. "Give me a few seconds."

She accessed her connection to the Mantle and the net, opening her bank account. In the Mantle, she scanned the virtual surroundings, until she found Frederick's persona nearby. She mentally poked it while saying, "Is this you?"

"Yep, that's me. Just wire the money there."

"Sending it now," Cass said.

Frederick pressed the button to raise the chair up again as Cass connected her bank account to Frederick's and sent five hundred dollars to him. Cass admitted to herself it was a lot easier than carrying a load of cash around with her.

"I'm glad to be of service, ladies. If you ever need anything again, don't hesitate to ask."

"I'll let my brother know what a good job you did. I'm sure he has other friends who need this kind of work done," Shelby said. She reached out for Cass's hand to help her stand up.

Cass turned back to Frederick. "Hey, how does this come off. I asked for a temporary version, so I assume it comes off somehow?"

"Just concentrate on the side of your face around the implant. The edges of the patch are tuned to you and will release on a signal from your implant. You'll see the connection points when you take it off. There are tiny magnets inside the patch holding it to your face around the implant. Pull on the edge and it'll automatically lift off so you can peel it away. To replace it, just hold it back in place and run your finger along the seam to create a fresh seal with your skin. The linkage and seal should hold up for six months to a year before it'll need to be replaced. A new one is only two hundred since I already have your personal template in my system."

"Sounds good. Thank you again," Cass said. She turned with Shelby and left. This solved one problem with her upcoming visit from her father. All she had to do was keep him away from Shelby and everything would be all right.

Chapter 17

FRIDAY ROLLED AROUND TOO QUICKLY for Cass. Despite the fact her new skin patch covered her implant perfectly, she was still apprehensive about meeting with her father.

Things were tense between herself and Shelby, too. Shelby wanted Cass to tell her father about Shelby's cybernetic enhancements, even if she didn't tell him about her own. Shelby told Cass she owed it to her parents to tell them the truth.

Cass knew Shelby had no idea how strong her parents' feelings were concerning cyber-humans. In the end, she convinced Shelby to go hang out with her brother all afternoon following her classes.

Shelby made her displeasure clear as she grabbed her purse and left that morning. Cass tried to talk to her to make her understand but Shelby refused to talk with her at all and left the room.

Cass checked the time via her implant and then went to scan her face in the mirror one last time before her father got there. She nodded. Nothing had changed so he should see nothing unusual. The skin patch matched and sealed to her skin just as it was designed to do.

Cass tugged at her wig, making sure it wouldn't come loose or shift while she was out to eat with her father. The portion of her implant that curved up and behind her ear was hidden by the wig. She'd be glad when her own hair grew back enough that she could get rid of the wig. It itched, especially on warm days like this.

There was a tap at her door. Cass knew it was her dad. The building's systems had already alerted her implant of his arrival when he checked in at the front desk.

She wondered again if that automaticity made her more susceptible to some sort of influence by the Mantle or a rogue AI. A chill ran down her spine as Cass thought about it.

Cass walked to the door, took a deep breath, and opened it. Her father greeted her with a big hug.

"Hi, honey. It's so good to see you in person again and not just on the other side of the screen."

"It's good to see you, too, Dad. Come on in."

Cass stepped back so her father could come into the room.

James Armstrong looked around the room and smiled. "It's nice of you to pick up for me."

"I know how to keep my room clean, Dad."

"Well, you'll have to make sure you clean up your room when you come home, too. It still looks like a cyclone hit it from when you left."

Cass resisted the urge to roll her eyes. She knew her dad was just trying his hand at some good-natured banter with her. He didn't mean anything by it.

"So, am I going to meet your girlfriend? I see she isn't here."

Cass hesitated for a second before answering. "No, Dad, Shelby is away with her family for the weekend. I wanted to have you all to myself."

The disappointment showed on James Armstrong's face as he frowned. Cass got the impression it wasn't only about meeting his daughter's girlfriend. She knew how suspicious her father was. He probably had tried to look up info on Shelby but had been unable to find anything. Cass had purposely given him misleading information so he wouldn't find out much about her on a routine search.

"I'm sorry, Dad. Something came up with her mom and she had to go away to deal with it."

"Never mind, hon. It's good to see you. You're the one I actually came to visit."

"How was your trip here?" Cass asked. "Did your business meetings go as planned this morning?"

"It did. We're concerned, though. There are several dissident groups in the city that we've heard are going to disrupt our perfectly legal march and rally. We've asked the chief of police and the city to turn down any requests for counter-demonstrations on the same weekend."

"Is that legal?" Cass asked. "Can't anyone apply for a permit to hold a demonstration?"

"Our movement has friends in high places all over the country. If those friends are not members of the movement outright, they're people who sympathize with us. One of them is the chief of police in the city. He's assured me that because those who've applied to date all have police records for various petty offenses, he has grounds to turn them down."

Cass wondered if Shelby's brother, Eric, was one of the dissidents her father referred to. She knew that not having the legal paperwork wasn't going to stop Eric. He and his friends would organize something whether he had a legal permit to hold a demonstration or not.

"The other reason I'm here, besides visiting you and helping to organize the march, is to talk with a few of the local legislators about a new bill we have coming up in the Congress. We're hoping to get some local support and a few new co-signers for the bill."

"What is the proposed law going to do?" Cass asked.

"It's going to make it illegal to make, produce, or manufacture any enhancements that are not specifically designed for medical uses."

Cass couldn't hide her surprise. "Really? Isn't that going a bit too far?"

"I'm surprised to hear you say that, Cass. You should know it doesn't go far enough. Still, it's a step in the right direction. If I had my way and thought we could push it through, we'd make sure that no implants could be manufactured that had connectivity to the

Mantle. These people need to be stopped for good or the AI is going to use them to take control of everyone."

"Do you think it'll pass?"

"I think it might. It's not everything I want but it's a step in the right direction. Allowing for medically necessary devices is a small price to pay given how few of them there are compared to the rampant use of black market implants around the country."

Hearing about the exception for medical devices made Cass feel like there might be some hope for her with her family. Maybe this meant she could let her parents know about what happened to her. Cass needed to talk to her father some more and figure out exactly how firmly he supported the stronger version of the bill. She'd bring it up again over dinner.

"So where are we going to dinner?" Cass asked.

"I thought I'd let you pick a place. You've been living here for several months. Surely you have a favorite restaurant by now."

"Yeah, I do. Honestly, though, Dad, I was hoping we could go somewhere a lot fancier than I can afford on my limited budget as a college student."

James laughed and smiled at his daughter. "Somehow, I knew you'd say something like that. No worries. I already talked to the police chief about it during our meeting. He recommended a nice steak and seafood house downtown. He even called ahead to make sure they had room for us. How does that sound to you?"

Cass nodded with enthusiasm. She hadn't had a decent steak since she'd come to college. The mystery meat they served in the cafeteria here on campus might be called steak, but it didn't taste like any steak she'd ever had before. "I think that would be awesome. Let me grab my purse and we can go."

Her dad walked over to the door and waited while she grabbed her purse from the side of her chair. Double checking to make sure the room was in order, Cass headed for the door.

"Don't forget your key," James said, pointing to the key card on the lanyard hanging from a hook next to her desk.

Cass stopped for a second, initially confused. She hadn't used a key card since her implant had been put in. Her door just recognized her and opened when she got there. She realized how close she had come to making a critical error.

"Oh yeah, thanks. I'd forget my head if it weren't attached." Cass walked over to her desk and grabbed the lanyard with the key card and slipped it into her bag.

Crossing back to the door, she gestured to her dad to lead the way. She let the door close behind her and latch as she and her father headed out to the dorm's common room. A few of Cass's friends said hi as she passed by. She smiled and returned the greetings then followed her father outside to the street. As expected, her father had rented a manually-operated car. He'd parked along the street nearby. As Cass climbed into the car, her father remarked on the rental.

"It's getting harder and harder to rent a car that isn't connected to the Mantle. They only had two on the whole lot when I landed. The clerk at the rental desk seemed to think the company wasn't buying any more like them in the future. I'm not sure what we're going to do about getting around after that. There's no way I'm trusting my life to a car operated by an AI."

Cass reached out with her mind. She saw right away this car had no external connection to the network around them. It was just a dumb machine.

"I'm sure there will be places that'll cater to your specific needs and people like us, Dad. Especially if some of the initiatives you've proposed to Mr. Noble go through."

"I hope so, Cassie. We need to get more people from the movement elected, first. That's in the plan for the next election cycle. Who knows? You might be out of school in time to work on a key congressional or senate campaign, maybe even a presidential campaign if we get Sterling the exposure he wants."

The thought of working on a presidential campaign alongside her father excited Cass. She realized, though, she'd have to have come clean about her implant by then. Maybe the position on medical devices would soften some once the new legislation passed.

As her dad steered them through traffic filled with automatic vehicles, their conversation turned to family news.

"Your mother was sorry she couldn't come along with me on this trip. She's really jealous that I get to see you and she doesn't."

"I'll make sure to call her this evening and spend extra time chatting with her. I know she's upset about not coming. I miss her, too. How's Elena doing?"

"Your sister is doing well in school. I think she's happy to be out from under your shadow. For a long time, she was known as Cass Armstrong's little sister. Now she has a chance to make a mark of her own as the only Armstrong in the school."

Cass was happy to hear her sister, Elena, was succeeding in her studies for a change. She'd always struggled in school before. Cass had always been the better student and athlete in the family.

"Is she involved in any activities at school?" Cass asked.

"She made the soccer team. She worked hard all summer before you left, as you know. I know you spent a lot of time with her on her skills. It paid off when tryouts came along. She's actually had some playing time and they seem to think she might move up from the JV squad to the varsity squad next year."

"I'm sorry I'm not going to be able to see her play."

"The school is actually recording the games and posting them on its restricted site. It doesn't have open access, but I think we can arrange to get you a password so you can have your own connection. I think she'd appreciate knowing that you were watching her games at least some of the time."

Cass nodded. "That would be nice. I'll send her a text when we get back to the room."

They arrived at the restaurant. It was every bit as nice as her father led her to believe.

"The police chief did a good job picking a place, Dad. This is great."

"It is. I'll be sure to thank him. We have one more follow-up meeting tomorrow over breakfast before I head home."

They sat down to eat and most of the conversation turned towards hearing updates about friends and family around the enclave.

As dinner ended, James drove Cass back to the dorm. It was just starting to get dark as they pulled up in front of the building. As Cass climbed out of the car, her dad froze. Two people walked by on the sidewalk. Cass wasn't sure what the problem was until she realized both people had implants.

The boy had an installation of monofilament fiber hair. The glowing filaments changed color as he walked down the sidewalk with his arm around a girl's waist. She had a metal ridge running up from her neck where it divided on either side to run up and over either ear. Her hair was shaved on the sides to show off the implants. The metal bars glowed with a deep purple light around the edges.

Cass overheard her father muttering under his breath. Her implant gave her better than average hearing. She easily heard him say, "damned subs."

"Hey, Dad, why don't you just drop me off here? That way you don't have to pay the parking meter again."

"That would actually be nice. I do need to start heading back to the hotel. I've got some calls to make tonight."

Cass walked around the front of the car to her father. She reached out and gave him a big hug.

"It's good to see you, Daddy."

"It's good to see you, too, cupcake. Make sure you continue to work hard on your studies. Finish strong." He said, starting the family motto.

"Armstrong," Cass replied, finishing the phrase.

Her words brought a smile to her father's face. He nodded and climbed into the car. Cass watched him drive away. She sighed. That had gone about as well as she could have hoped. Now, to head in and apologize to Shelby.

Chapter 18

WHEN CASS RETURNED, Shelby sat waiting on her bed.

"So, how did it go?" Shelby asked.

"It went all right," Cass replied with a shrug. "He hasn't changed at all, not that I expected him to."

"You knew he wasn't going to be any different, Cass. He hasn't given you any indication during your face chats that his opinion has changed on anything."

"I know, but I keep hoping he'll soften in some way. He talked some about a new piece of legislation going before Congress."

"What's it going to do?"

Cass hesitated before answering. "It's going to outlaw any manufacture or installation of cyber enhancements on humans outside of medically necessary implants."

"They can't do that," Shelby exclaimed. "People have a right to do what they want with their bodies."

"He made a point to say there'd be an exception made for medical needs. He wasn't happy about that concession, but he saw the need for it."

"What about the rally my brother heard about?" Shelby asked.

"There is one planned. He's working with the police chief to shut down any counter-protests by refusing their permits."

"I have to tell my brother," Shelby said. "He knew there was going to be a rally, but he didn't know about this. If they restrict counter-protests, it changes everything."

"Be careful what you tell him, Shelby. No one's supposed to know about this. If something crops up here on campus, Dad might think I told somebody."

"Nonsense, he won't suspect you. He's had meetings with people about this all day. He'll think one of them, or one of their assistants, leaked something to someone."

"Maybe. I think Eric should be careful, though. This rally and the pending legislation are going to happen. My father was pretty adamant about it."

Shelby didn't answer her and Cass glanced in her roommate's direction. Shelby had stood up. She stared over Cass's shoulder at the door to their room behind her. They left it open when they were just hanging out, so people could come by and visit.

A horrible feeling filled Cass with dread as she turned around.

James Armstrong said, "Your father is adamant about what, Cass?"

"Dad, what are you doing here? I thought you were leaving."

"I forgot to give you something from your mother." James Armstrong held out a package wrapped in brown paper. "It's a new sweater she thought you would enjoy since the weather was getting colder. She'd kill me if I forgot to give it to you."

James looked past Cass at Shelby. He couldn't disguise the disgust on his face. With a sneer, he said, "Who's your friend, Cass?"

"This is Shelby, Dad."

"This. Is. Shelby." Her father said, enunciating each word.

Cass realized he was at a loss for words for the first time in her life. He stammered a few times as if starting to say something else.

Her father found his voice at last as he took a step forward pointing at Shelby. Anger twisted his face as he said, "What have you done with my daughter? She'd never let someone like you anywhere near her. Come on, tell me what you did to her to make her take a freak like you to bed?"

Cass slid to the side and stood in front of her father, inserting herself between him and Shelby. "She didn't do anything to me, Dad. I am still the same. I just learned that everything is not exactly how you said it is."

"You don't know everything I know, Cass. Haven't we taught you? Haven't we warned you enough? People like her aren't human anymore. They don't have emotions. They don't love. They've become machines. You can't trust them."

"Don't say that about her, Dad. I love her."

James Armstrong laughed out loud. "How can you love a machine? That's what she is, you know. She gave up her humanity when she became a thing connected to the Mantle."

Shelby jumped to Cass's defense. "I'm a human just like your daughter is Mr. Armstrong. You have no idea who I am or what I've been through. I have every right to do what I want with my body. It doesn't make me any less human."

James turned away from Shelby to look at Cass. "I don't talk to machines. She's nothing but an AI pawn. Cassidy, I'm so disappointed in you. How could you let this sub into your life?"

"Don't call her that."

"I'll call her what she is. She's sub-human. I thought I raised you to understand these things. I'm calling the police. It's clear to me she has some sort of unnatural influence over you."

Cass reached out and grabbed her father's hand as he reached into his jacket pocket for his phone. "That's enough, Dad. You can't treat people that way. Shelby is my girlfriend. She's as human as I am. If you can't accept that, then you need to leave."

James stared at Cass for a few seconds, glanced over her shoulder at Shelby once, then turned and walked to the door.

When he reached the doorway, he stopped and turned to look back at Cass. "I'm going to contact the college president. I happen to know he has some sympathy in our direction. I'm going to make sure he moves you to another room. A room that doesn't have an infestation in it like this one."

"Daddy, I'm not moving anywhere."

"We'll see about that. I'm not going to tell your mother about this. It would destroy her. We'll take care of it between us."

"Why not tell Mom?" Cass said. "Are you afraid she'll side with me?"

"No, I'm afraid she'll be heartbroken. You were always her favorite. I'm afraid she's going to disown you over this, Cass. I understand you're not yourself right now. That can be fixed once we get you home at the end of the semester. You're finished here at this school. Your mother's opinion of you can't be fixed so easily. I'd rather she didn't know you took one of these things to your bed."

Shelby came up behind beside Cass and put an arm around her shoulder. "You can call me what you want, Mr. Armstrong. I have done nothing to your daughter except care for her and show her how much I love her. If you can't accept that, then you should leave. You can't stay in this dorm if we don't want you here. We can have you ejected."

Cass turned and stared at Shelby. She knew technically, Shelby was correct. She didn't think it would be something Shelby would ever do. Now, however, she wasn't sure.

Cass turned back to her father. Having security come and throw him out would only make things worse if that was even possible. "Dad, Shelby is right, I think you should leave. If you want, we can talk about this in the morning before you leave. I'm not moving from this room, though. You'll have to deal with how mom responds when you get home tomorrow. I'm going to call her when you leave. She deserves to hear about it from me, not you when you're worked up like this."

James started to say something, stopped himself, and shook his head. Without another word, he turned around and left.

Cass stared at the empty doorway for a long time after her father disappeared down the hallway. She monitored his progress all the way out of the building via her implant. Shelby walked over and closed the door.

As the latch clicked shut, Cass turned and fell to her bed, collapsing on it as the tears began to flow. After the dinner with her father had went so well, after she'd managed to hide her own implant from her dad, everything still fell apart. Why hadn't she closed the door when she came in the room?

Shelby came over and sat next to her and leaned over to hold Cass close as she continued crying. "It's going to be all right, Cass. You'll see. Your father can't control you anymore. You've proven him wrong. You've proven everything he's ever taught you is wrong."

Cass pulled away from Shelby. "It's not that simple, Shelby. I don't necessarily disagree with everything he believes in. I've learned that some of the things he taught me about the world are not what they seem to be, but that doesn't mean everything I was raised to understand is wrong."

"How can you say that when you just saw how he reacted to me?"

"Shelby, I came to your defense. I told him to leave."

"Then how can you say that you still believe anything that man and others like him believe?"

"Because I'm not going to just change everything overnight. I'm not the same person I was when I got here, that's true. Still, I'm going to be my own person and form my own opinions about things."

"Well, you better figure this out, Cass. Your father is not going to make things easy on us. He's right about one thing. I know the college president isn't a sympathizer to people like me. He can make our lives difficult if he wants to."

"I'm not necessarily sure what we can do. I'm going to make sure he doesn't separate us, though."

"Let me talk to my brother," Shelby said. "He's already been through school here. He might have some insights into how we can navigate this."

"You do that. I need to get on face chat with my mom and talk to her about this before Dad does."

"Do you want me to sit with you while you call her?" Shelby asked. "I don't mind. I won't say anything. I promise. At least you can introduce us."

"No, you go and talk to Eric. That's important too."

"Okay, but I'll be nearby if you need me for anything."

Cass nodded. She wondered whether she should tell her mom about her own enhancements, too. Perhaps it was best to come clean about everything at once. Cass shook her head and decided it was better to take things one step at a time. She'd gauge her mother's response as she talked with her.

She picked up her tablet and tapped the icon connecting her to her home.

Her sister Elena answered. Elena's face filled the screen. Her dark brown curls framed her face as she leaned close to the camera.

"Hey sis," Elena said. "What did you do to Dad? He's on the phone with Mom. He sounds pissed. I could hear him yelling even without it being on speaker."

"That's why I'm calling. He and I had a fight about something and I need to talk to Mom about it."

Elena looked over her shoulder and then back at the screen. "I think she's going to be on the line with him for a while. Do you want to talk to me instead? You can, you know."

Cass considered it for a few seconds before answering. "You know what, you're right. I can tell you. Maybe you can help get through to Mom and Dad for me before I have to come back home."

"Wow, it must be pretty serious. Don't worry sis, I've got your back."

"It's about my girlfriend, Shelby."

"Did Dad meet her finally?"

"Yeah, and she's not the type of person he's inclined to accept in my life."

A puzzled frown crossed Elena's face. "What do you mean?"

"I guess maybe you should meet her," Cass said. "Then you'll understand."

Shelby had been listening. She came over and sat down next to Cass so she could be in the video's frame with her girlfriend.

Elena's eyes widened on the other side of the connection, taking it all in. "You're dating a sub? No wonder Dad's so pissed."

Cass's anger boiled to the surface. "Don't call her that. Don't ever call her that. She's my girlfriend. You don't know anything about her. People with enhancements aren't what you think they are, Elena. They're not what anybody taught us about them. They're people just like us."

Elena was silent for a long time, staring at Cass and Shelby through the screen. Eventually, she found her voice.

"This explains why Dad is upset. Mom's not going to be happy either. Look, Cassie, I'm sorry I said what I said. It caught me by surprise. Hi, Shelby. I'm Elena."

"It's nice to meet you, Elena. I've been after Cass to introduce me to you all for a while. I'm looking forward to getting to know you. I don't have a little sister of my own."

Elena smiled, then frowned again. "Um, I guess I should apologize to you, too. I shouldn't have called you that word."

"It's just how you were raised, Elena. Hopefully, I can help you understand that things are different from what you've been taught."

Elena didn't say anything in response and everyone fell into silence again. Cass realized that her little sister was processing a lot right then. She didn't want Elena to get caught in the middle of this. That wasn't fair when she was stuck home with their parents alone.

"Elena, listen to me. I changed my mind. I don't want you to get between me and Mom and Dad. Just tell Mom I called and ask her to face chat me when she gets a chance. If you want to run interference in the background without letting on you know anything, that's fine, but don't do anything to bring their wrath down on you. Understand?"

"I understand. I can take care of myself, Cassie. Things have been different since you left. Mom and Dad seem to actually like me for a change."

"They've always liked you, Squirt," Cass said. "You just felt like you couldn't be your own person with me around. I'm sorry if I made that worse for you. Hopefully, now that I am gone most of the time, things will lighten up."

"They already have," Elena said.

"Good. I'm glad. Look, I'm going to go. Make sure you get Mom to call as soon as she gets a chance."

Elena nodded and then reached out and closed the connection on her end.

Shelby turned to Cass as the screen went blank. "I don't know your sister, Cass, but she seemed okay with us once she got over the initial shock. Is that a good sign? Does this mean she's on our side?"

"I think so," Cass said the words. Inside, though, she wasn't so sure. She and her sister had always been rivals in many ways. Even so, growing up she'd felt like she could rely on Elena to help her when she really needed her to. She liked to think she could count on her now.

"Let's hope my mom calls soon. I don't think Dad's going to talk to her that long."

"Don't worry, Cass," Shelby said, holding her close. "I'll be here with you the whole time. Moms sometimes have a way of getting around the problems people have in their families. I know my mom always comes back to me after we have a fight."

"I hope so. Somehow, though, I think this might be different."

Chapter 19

CASS'S MOTHER never did call her back. Initially, it upset her. The more she thought about the whole situation, though, the angrier she got with her parents. The one good thing that had come from the argument with her dad was how it solidified some things in her mind that had been altered for a while. Her father's reaction to Shelby was ugly and born of an irrational fear of something he didn't understand.

That revelation helped Cass see that perhaps there was a way she could help fight against such misconceptions. She now understood where both sides came from. Maybe she could somehow bridge the gap between the two viewpoints to show them the error of their ways with both extremes.

She knew Eric was planning a counter-demonstration for the upcoming Sapiens rally. Based on some of his comments, she got the impression from him that he'd show up with or without a permit to march. That could lead to violence. Cass hoped by getting involved, she could change that.

She broached the subject with Shelby at breakfast the next day.

"Shelby, can you get in touch with your brother for me?"

"Sure, what for?"

"I think I'd like to volunteer to help out with the upcoming counter-rally to the Sapiens march."

Shelby smiled. "Cass, that's wonderful. I can't believe you decided to do something like that. It's a huge step."

"Don't misunderstand me, Shelby. I'm doing this because I think there's a place in the middle for both sides to meet. I kind of hope that I can help steer Eric in the right direction to that middle ground."

Shelby shook her head. "I don't know, Cass. My brother is passionate about this, much more so than I am. I know how I feel about the Sapiens party line. He's a hundred times more committed to the cause of eradicating everything the Sapiens stand for."

"Maybe if I talk to him about how I grew up, he'd understand we're not all horrible people. Most of us are just people like you. Maybe we learned some things that weren't true. It doesn't mean we can't learn when confronted with the truth. If there's some sort of violent confrontation, no one wins and everyone thinks the worst of the others."

"I guess it doesn't hurt to try talking with him. I know he'll listen to your side better than your father did."

"I hope so. Because I'm not going to be as patient with him as I was with my father."

"You were patient with your father?" Shelby asked with a laugh. "Please don't try to use that kind of patience with me, okay?"

"I promise," Cass said with a smile. "I guess I got a little angry with Dad last night."

"You could say that," Shelby agreed. She reached across the table and grasped Cass's hand. "I've never seen you like that. It was kind of nice the way you came to my defense. I liked it."

Cass smiled and leaned over to place her other hand atop Shelby's. She gave it a gentle squeeze. "I didn't like the way he talked to you. He had no right to treat you that way. He doesn't know you the way I do and he doesn't understand what I've learned since we've been together."

"You have to accept the fact he may never understand," Shelby said. "I know I told you they might accept your implants. Now that

I've met him, I don't think he's going to change, Cass. No matter what you do or how hard you try to show him, he may never come around or even believe you're the same Cassie he raised. He may not be the person you thought he was before all of this."

Cass sat still, staring past Shelby for a moment as she processed her girlfriend's words. She didn't like what they suggested. She didn't want to think her father was intractable and unable to change when faced with evidence he was wrong.

Cass decided to change the subject. "Shel, even if my father will never come around, I still want to help out some with the counter-protest. I think it's important to stand up for what we believe in and who we are."

"Cass, getting involved actively to oppose your father this way isn't exactly what I meant when I said you need to stand up to him. If he finds out, he'll be furious, won't he?"

Cass nodded. "He will but I also think he's already angry at me. It's time somebody stood up to him. Maybe that someone has to be me."

She reached up and touched her face where the skin patch still adhered to her cheek from the night before, covering her implant. Cass ran her finger along the seam. As she did, the patch's edge lifted up. She grabbed it with her forefinger and thumb and peeled it away, placing it in the plastic case Frederick had given her for it. Cass put the plastic case in her purse.

"Come on, let's go for a walk, Shel. We can try and talk about something fun for a change, like our upcoming finals in a month."

"Haha, very funny. I, for one, would rather talk about anything but finals. You're right, though. It's a good idea for us to get out, get some fresh air, and be around people who aren't judging us all the time."

The two of them got up and left the cafeteria together. Cass cherished the way her hand felt in Shelby's as they walked along. She'd had only one serious relationship before, in high school, but that didn't begin to approach the level of feeling she had for Shelby. She loved this dynamic, passionate woman and would do anything for her.

Later that evening, after classes, Shelby reached out to contact Eric on Cass's behalf. As the face chat opened and Shelby greeted her brother, Cass came over to sit next to her girlfriend to join in the conversation.

"Hey bro," Shelby said. "Cass wanted to ask you something and I thought it would be important enough to check in with you as soon as possible."

"You know it's never a problem to chat with my little sister or the person attached to her right hip. What's up, Cass?"

"Well, I thought that maybe I could help out in some way with your upcoming rallies. It's something I think is important for me to do right now."

Eric's eyebrows shot up in surprise. "Really, because I would think somebody with your connection to the Sapiens movement would want to keep a low profile."

"That was before my father decided to say something nasty about your sister. I think people need to understand something about people who have grown up the way I did. We can change. Showing that is important. We all need to talk to each other to help foster understanding. Maybe doing it through an open and public rally is the way to go."

"I think that would be great, Cass. If you want to jump in right away, there's an event coming up this weekend. It's a precursor to the main one in two weeks. We want to raise awareness for our cause before those bigoted bastards come and march through our city."

"Eric," Shelby said, interrupting her brother. "Some of them are Cass's family and friends. They're not all evil. I met her sister and she seemed nice. Cass is trying to show you they're not all the people you think they are."

"You're right. Sorry, Sis."

"Don't apologize to me."

"Yeah, um, sorry, Cass."

"It's okay, Eric. This is why it's important I join you guys. You all need to understand something about who the people on the other side are and why they believe the things they do."

"Fair enough," Eric said. "Why don't you and Shelby come down and rally with us this Saturday morning downtown on Water Street, just off the square in front of City Hall. That's where we'll be holding our event. It's near the Bizarre. We are protesting some recent measures brought up before the City Council by the mayor to extend police initiatives to shut down enhancements when cyber-humans are arrested or taken into custody."

"That's horrible," Cass said. "How can they do that? It would be like taking someone's arm or leg off and then putting them in a cage. In Cass's case, it would kill her."

Eric nodded. "That's exactly the way we all feel, too. You understand us now, Cass. I wish it hadn't happened the way it did, but I'm glad you have had this revelation. I'll send you the final details on the time and place we're meeting in the morning Saturday as soon as we iron out our permits and stuff."

"That would be awesome," Shelby said. "Cass and I are looking forward to helping out any way we can."

"You should both know, however, there is a chance the police will get involved, breaking up our demonstration. There have been rumblings that they are not going to let us have a rally at all. We still haven't gotten word of approval for the demonstration from the city. No matter what they say, we're going to hold it anyway."

Cass considered what he said. She'd never had any kind of dealings with the police before. She'd always been taught that they were there to protect others and to help people. Something about the way Eric referred to them hinted that he'd had different experiences. That was something else she could help with.

"We'll be fine," Cass said, looking at Shelby for reassurance. "It's time I got more involved. If there are risks to that, then so be it."

"All right, then. I guess that means I'll see you on Saturday. If you can't make it, let me know. Otherwise, I'll see you this weekend."

"See you, Bro," Shelby said as she reached out to cut the connection. She turned to Cass with a huge smile on her face. "I'm so proud of you, Cass."

"I'm not trying to do something to make you proud, though that is a nice side effect. I'm trying to do what's right and stand up for something I believe in."

"Well, whatever the reason, I am proud of you. We're going to have a blast at this rally. You're going to see a lot of other folks just like you."

"I hope so," Cass said. "That would be great. It's time I got involved and learned about who I am now."

Chapter 20

AS CASS HEADED downtown with Shelby to meet up with Eric on Saturday morning, she wasn't sure what to expect from the coming rally. She and Shelby were dressed for cold weather. It wasn't going to rain, which was good, but it was going to be a bit windy. Both wore coats, hats, and scarves against the early morning chill.

Eric arranged for all of the rally attendees to meet in the underground area of the Bizarre. The marketplace hadn't officially opened yet and the vendors hadn't arrived. Everyone was able to spread out and assist each other in assembling the placards and signs they were to carry during the demonstration.

Cass and Shelby worked at stapling the cardboard signs Eric had printed up to long wooden slats so they could be carried by the demonstrators.

Most of the signs were focused on encouraging new laws for broader rights and protections for cyber-humans under current constitutional provisions. A few were also aimed directly at calling out Sapiens movement members as racists and bigots. Those were the signs that made Cass uncomfortable when she first read them.

Shelby must've seen Cass glancing at the girl next to them. She had assembled a bunch of those anti-Sapiens signs.

She nudged Cass's elbow to draw her attention back to what they were working on. "Don't worry. You won't have to carry one of those signs if you don't want to."

"It's just a little bit of a shock. Six months ago, I would have fallen under that description. It's as much a stereotype as what the other side believes. I never considered myself bigoted before now."

"You're more open to learning about and respecting others," Shelby said. "You were open enough to change your view about me before you had your accident. After everything you've been through, you've become more open about how you see yourself now, too."

Cass shook her head. "But what kind of person would I have been if I had not been injured? What does that say about who I was before I became a cyber-human?"

"You're still adjusting to everything, Cass. Heck, you're still healing from your injury. Try not to push yourself to get too used to it all too quickly."

Cass finished stapling the sign they were working on and set it off to the side with a stack of others. "I hope so. I still don't feel a hundred percent like myself. I'm not even sure what that means anymore."

"Change is inevitable, Cass. We all change. You're not going to be the same person you were five minutes ago. We're always becoming something different, hopefully for the better."

"Except for my dad," Cass remarked. "He hasn't changed at all. Now, I don't think he ever will."

"Don't worry about him. He doesn't have to rule your life anymore."

Cass didn't answer. She didn't think Shelby understood how much her father controlled so many aspects of her life. He paid for her tuition. He made it so that she could live a comfortable life while she went to school. He could take all that away from her if he wanted to.

Eric happened by at that moment. "Signs look great, ladies. I'm glad you all came early to help out. I think everyone is just about finished up, so gather up what you've done and let's head out to the street. The rest of the demonstrators are starting to show up and we can start handing out the signs to people."

Cass and Shelby stood up. Each of them bent over and picked up a stack of signs. Cass hadn't realized they'd made so many.

"Wow, Shelby, we might have to make a couple of trips to get all these upstairs."

"They're not that heavy. It won't take us that long." Cass and Shelby followed the others from the underground garage up the stairs and into the alley before heading out to the street nearby.

The number of people gathered there surprised Cass. Everywhere she looked, she saw people with all varieties of enhancements and augmentations. Some of them she remembered seeing from her trip to the Bizarre the first time. Others were even more unique. There was even a woman walking around on long leg extensions. She had to be nearly eight feet tall.

Cass and Shelby set their signs down in a pile next to others. People came by to take the signs while the two of them went back downstairs and gathered up the rest they'd made.

"Looks like we'll make it in two trips," Shelby said. "Make sure you remember to save one for yourself."

"I will. This is all kind of exciting, Shel. I'm glad Eric was able to obtain the permit for the March."

Shelby shot Cass a look. "He wasn't. Whatever gave you the idea he did?"

"I just assumed since we had all these printed signs and things that he'd gotten some sort of official permission to move forward. You mean he didn't get the permit from the mayor and city hall?"

Shelby shook her head. "No, that's why it's even more important this demonstration happens. They are trying to keep us quiet. We can't afford to let them silence us. We have just as much a right to have a rally day as everyone else does."

Cass didn't answer right away. Her mind was swimming in thoughts of how she'd gotten wrapped up in doing something that might be illegal. She had never even stolen a candy bar in her entire life. The idea that someone would intentionally go against the law was alien to her.

Shelby took one look at her and laughed. "Good grief, Cass. You're pale as a sheet. Don't be that way. Everything's going to be just fine. What are they going to do, lock up everyone standing out here on the street? They won't have enough room in the jail if they do that."

"That's not necessarily a reassuring thing to say," Cass replied. "If they wanted to lock everyone up, I'm sure they'd find a way to accommodate us."

"You worry too much. Come on. Let's get upstairs before they march off without us."

They carried the final load of signs upstairs and got there in time to hand them out to the remaining people in the street. Cass wasn't good at estimating numbers in a crowd, but she figured there had to be at least a thousand people there. They filled the street for an entire city block.

Eric's voice sounded over a loudspeaker from the front of the march. "All right, let's get started. Remember that our chant is 'cyber rights, right now.' Let's try it together. One, two, three!"

The crowd shouted out as soon as he finished counting. "Cyber rights, right now! Cyber rights, right now."

Everyone cheered and raised their fists above their heads along with their signs.

"Well done, let's start heading towards City Hall and let them know that we won't be silenced. Let them hear our voices as we call out for justice."

With Eric's words, the marchers started down the street. They were about a kilometer away from City Hall.

It was going to be a beautiful morning. Despite the chill, the sun was shining and the breeze from earlier had died down. Cass's excitement overcame her apprehension and soon she shouted and chanted along with all the rest as she and Shelby marched side-by-side down the street.

They hadn't gone more than a couple of blocks before they saw the first sign of a police presence. Cass saw police cars blocking the side streets as they passed by. At first, Cass thought the police cars were there to keep side street traffic from interfering with the marchers.

Then she spotted a group of police with helmets and clear plastic shields in the next cross street gathered behind the line of police cars. A nagging worry began tickling the back of her mind. Those armored police officers were dressed for more than traffic control and now she thought the police cars looked more like they were positioned to keep the demonstrators in, not passing cars out.

"The police seem to be trying to herd us in one particular direction," Cass said to Shelby as they marched along. She glanced over her shoulder. A police department van now followed behind them, moving slowly but keeping pace with the marchers.

"They're just here to make sure we don't start breaking things or destroying property," Shelby said. "They think we're just here to be trouble-makers. They don't understand what we really want."

Cass shook her head. "It doesn't look like they want to find out. Why would they bring a van or dress in riot gear for something like this unless they planned on arresting a bunch of people?"

"You're just being paranoid, Cass. Keep marching and stay with the group. There's safety in numbers. We'll be fine."

Cass kept going but continued watching the encroachment of the police while she walked at Shelby's side.

They almost reached the point where they were to make a left turn up the main boulevard towards City Hall when things started slowing down. Cass and Shelby were towards the back of the demonstrators and couldn't see what the hold-up was. There seemed to be something going on up at the front of the march.

"Can you see what's going on up there?" Cass asked Shelby. "I thought maybe with your height you could see over the crowd."

"I can't see anything. Maybe if you get up higher, you can make out something with your telescopic vision."

"I can try. I can't see over everyone's head, though. Let's move to the sidewalk. Maybe I can stand on something to see over the crowd."

Together, Shelby and Cass started working their way between the other demonstrators towards the side of the street. Everyone was still shouting and pressed forward, packing tighter and tighter towards the front.

Shelby and Cass reached the sidewalk and Cass stepped up onto the concrete base of a light pole. She could see something going on at the front of the group. There was some sort of commotion, but she wasn't sure what it was.

Cass concentrated, focusing on using her ocular implant for the first time in full telephoto mode. The events unfolding at the front of the group expanded and zoomed into focus until it was as if she were standing right there.

She spotted Eric at the front with the other leaders of the march. They'd stopped and faced a line of police in riot gear with clear plastic shields, helmets, and clubs like the police Cass had seen behind them in the side streets.

The line of police officers blocked the street so the marchers couldn't make the turn towards City Hall. Eric shouted at the police officers. He raised his fist in defiance towards the police while he called out to encourage those around him.

"Shelby, the police blocked the street ahead. Eric is up there with the others, but they can't move forward. The cops are all spread out in front of them with riot gear."

"They're coming in behind us too," Shelby said pointing to the rear.

Cass turned to look. Shelby was correct. A double line of police officers, all decked out with helmets and shields, filed in from two side streets behind them. That police line started moving forward towards the rear of the marchers. Most hadn't noticed them coming yet.

"Shelby, we need to get out of here. I have a bad feeling about this."

"We have to get up to the front and help my brother. He doesn't know we're surrounded. He won't back down unless he realizes they've beaten us."

"I don't think there's going to be anywhere to retreat to if we don't get out of here now," Cass said. "The police don't look like they're leaving anywhere for us to go."

The demonstrators in the back of the march started to notice the approaching police behind them. Some of them turned and started shouting at the advancing police officers. Cass knew that wouldn't solve anything. The police officers were just doing their jobs. The marchers didn't have a permit to be here.

The line of officers now penned in the marchers so they were trapped on the street inside one city block between dual lines of armored police officers.

Cass hopped down from the concrete base of the light post. "Shelby, there's no place for us to run. They've blocked the street in both directions now. We need to stop shouting at them and surrender. Fighting against them isn't going to solve anything."

Shelby looked around and shook her head. "I don't know. We need to find a way out. We can try to go into one of these buildings. Maybe the doors are unlocked. It's still pretty early on a Saturday. Most of these stores aren't open yet."

Cass ran up to the front steps of a small apartment building. The door was locked. Cass pulled at the handle several times anyway to try and get inside. Several other demonstrators saw what she did and they also started checking for open doors in the buildings on that side of the street.

"We're trapped," a woman in front of the next building yelled.

As soon as the woman said it, the police started pressing forward even faster and the first tear gas canisters flew through the air to land in the midst of the crowd. Cass saw one of the gas grenades strike a woman with glowing, rainbow-colored filaments on her head. The canister cut open the skin on her forehead and knocked her down and out of sight. Cass couldn't see if she got back up again or not because Shelby pulled her down from the step and pointed up the street towards the front of the marchers.

"Let's head in that direction. Maybe we can slip around the line of police and get away that way."

Cass followed Shelby. They ran up the sidewalk, pressing their way between the other demonstrators.

Panic set in among the marchers as more tear gas grenades landed in the crowd from the line of police in the front. People started running in every direction to try to get away from the advancing police officers. Unfortunately, there was nowhere to go.

The smoke from the tear gas filled the street and sidewalk. Cass began coughing. Her human eye teared up and burned. She shut it to try and keep the gas from irritating it anymore. Shelby stumbled in front of her, her eyes closed against the gas, too.

Cass's ocular implant still worked, though. It was impervious to the gas.

Cass reached out to her girlfriend. "Here, Shelby, hold my hand. Stay with me. I'll try to get us out of here."

"Cass, try to see if you can spot Eric. I need to know he's okay."

It was impossible to see anything farther than a few feet away anymore. Police officers advanced forward into the demonstrators, pressing the crowd back with their shields. As they knocked people down, officers behind the initial line of police dragged the demonstrators away with their hands secured behind their backs. Several police vans sat waiting with the rear doors open.

"They're arresting everyone, Shelby. They're not letting anyone out. There's no sign of Eric anywhere."

Shelby panicked and pulled at Cass's arm. "We have to get out of here. If we get arrested, too, we'll never be able to help Eric."

Cass kept moving forward, hoping for a break in the police line, allowing the two of them to push through and get away.

They weren't so lucky.

The police kept advancing and, before Cass knew it, two police officers raised their riot clubs up right in front of her.

Cass raised her arm over her head and crouched down with Shelby to the sidewalk. "Please don't hit us."

"On your knees. Put your hands behind your back. Do it now, or so help me I'll knock you down myself." The police officer shouted at the two women. Cass was struck by the anger in his eyes.

Shelby and Cass fell to their knees and ducked their heads down, trying to comply with the police officer's orders.

Hands grabbed Cass's wrists, yanking them awkwardly backward until she cried out in pain. They secured her hands behind her back with flexible plastic ties, jerked tight around her hands and wrists.

Once she was secured, they grabbed her by her elbows and hauled Cass to her feet. She and Shelby were half-walked, half-dragged towards a large open van at the corner.

"Why are you doing this?" Cass asked the police officer pulling her forward. "We were being peaceful. We didn't hurt anyone."

"Shut up," the policeman to her left said. "You subs were told to stay away from City Hall. You were told you weren't allowed to hold this little demonstration. You are the ones who broke the law and now you're going to pay for it."

The officers dragged Cass and Shelby forward until they reached the van and shoved the two of them into the back. They slid forward on their knees until they reached more people huddling inside near the front of the compartment.

They sat there staring out the back of the van as officers brought more people over. Soon the van was full. The door closed with a clang. Cass heard the door latch click from the outside. There was very little light inside the van but Cass was able to see better than most, thanks to her ocular implant. A few people bled from cuts on their heads and faces. She couldn't see anyone who was seriously injured though. Eric wasn't among the demonstrators in the van with them.

The van jerked forward, driving away from the site of the demonstration. All Cass and Shelby could do was hold onto each other as the police took them away.

Chapter 21

THE POLICE VAN finally stopped and the doors popped open. Cass struggled to hold back her tears as the police officers at the rear of the van barked orders at them to hurry up and climb out. She tried to hold on to Shelby, but an officer yanked the two of them apart. The women and men were separated into two lines.

"Let go of your girly," one woman said. "You can't go in together. Everyone gets processed separately."

"But ..." Cass started to say.

"Are you arguing with me?" the female officer said. She was even taller than Shelby and towered over Cass. She stabbed a finger at Cass, poking her in the chest, forcing her to back up.

"I'm sorry," Cass said, trying to twist away. "I'll listen. Please stop poking me."

"Follow instructions and get back in line. Move forward one at a time for processing."

Cass nodded and stepped forward. At this point, Shelby was already about ten people ahead of her in line. She thought for a moment about trying to cut in front of the others to catch up to her, but the police officer still watched her. She feared what would happen if she got out of line again.

She waited her turn as they moved forward. When she finally reached the door and stepped inside, there was a small counter with another female police officer seated behind it.

"Empty your pockets. Put everything you have on the counter."

Cass followed instructions. She only had a data chip from school and her credit chip ID on her. She put both of those on the counter

The policewoman slid the credit ID into a reader, glanced at the screen, and then back at Cass. The woman pulled her credit ID out of the reader, dropped it in a clear plastic envelope with the other data chip, and put it in a pile with separate envelopes. A label with a bar code printed out. The officer slapped it on top.

Cass realized that was her now. She wasn't even a name to these people, just a bar code and a number.

"Move along to the next room for your mug shot." There, another female police officer sounded just as bored with the litany.

Based upon the number of people who'd been in line ahead of Cass she'd probably said it fifty times already.

Cass moved forward into the next room. Hands grabbed her and pushed her up against the wall in front of a backdrop marked with different heights to measure her in the photo.

A flash of light told her they'd taken the picture. She blinked against the bright light.

An officer stepped up next to her with a black metal tube in his hand. Cass flinched as he raised it up next to her head.

"Hold still."

"What are you doing?"

"Regulations say you can't have your implant active while in custody."

"But, mine is medically necessary."

"Don't worry, it will only shut down non-essential systems. We can't have you using your Mantle connection on the inside."

Before Cass could protest again, a blinding pain seared through her head. Her vision went dark in her right, artificial eye and dizziness threatened to make her fall.

Her thoughts became jumbled and she couldn't remember where she was and why she was here.

"Where am I? What are you doing to me?" Cass protested.

"Shut up and keep moving towards the cells."

Cass stumbled forward. Her legs weren't working. She realized it was all because her implant was no longer working. She tried to push through the fog over her mind to think about what to do next.

She joined a group of five other women. They were all placed in a cell already near capacity. There was nowhere to sit but the floor.

"Cass, over here," Shelby called from across the room.

Cass limped over, forcing her legs to work despite the fog clouding her mind.

Shelby jumped up from where she sat and pulled Cass into a one-armed embrace.

Tears flowed, from both of them although Cass tried to hold them back and said, "Shelby, what are we going to do?"

"We're going to sit here and follow instructions until it's our turn to make a few calls and get bailed out," Shelby said it all as if this was something she did every weekend.

"Who am I going to call?" Cass asked. "I can't call my father and I don't think your parents are going to bail me out."

"Don't worry, Cassie," Shelby said. "We'll work something out. Here, you sit down. I think they affected something when they deactivated your implant. Mine just shut down my v-tats and left arm. It'll all be okay. They'll start processing us through for bail soon enough."

Cass sat down and looked around the room at the other demonstrators in the lockup. She recognized a few faces from the morning's work group in the Bizarre. Most of the other inmates were strangers to her, though. She realized how odd it was that she was here. She'd made a spur of the moment decision to help out with the demonstration earlier that week and now she found herself in jail.

Shelby was right about the wait before bail arrangements could be made. A few male police officers came in and started processing each of them one at a time.

The officers took turns. They'd come into the hallway outside of the cell, call out a name, then take the person out and down the hall into the central police station. Sometimes the person was brought back after a few minutes, other times, the officer would return without the prisoner and call someone else.

Cass figured that bail was being paid for those who could arrange it. The guards called them by last name only and sorted it out at the gate if there was more than one with the same last name.

When they came to call Cass, though, it was different. An older officer they hadn't seen before came in and called out for Cass by her full given name.

"Cassidy Anne Armstrong," the police officer called out. He had the three stripes of a sergeant on his shoulder.

Cass stood up. "I'm Cassidy Armstrong."

"Come to the door, Miss," the sergeant said.

When she hesitated, he smiled at her and nodded as if to offer her reassurance. He seemed nicer than the other officers.

"Come along now, Miss. There's been a mix-up. You weren't supposed to get picked up with everyone else."

Cass didn't understand what was going on, but she followed instructions moving to the cell door. The sergeant gave a nod to another police officer standing there. He unlocked the barred gate to let her out.

When Cass stepped through into the hallway, she turned to look back at Shelby. Shelby smiled back at her and nodded. She mouthed the word "go."

Cass turned and looked at the sergeant. "What's this all about. Am I supposed to call someone to arrange bail?"

"Come with me. That's all you need to know right now. Everything's been arranged."

The sergeant's instructions confused Cass. She complied with the officer's orders, however, and fell in behind him. They walked down the hallway and through the door into the main part of the police station.

The sergeant led her to a desk where she saw a clear envelope with the bar code and number assigned to her. She knew this because her name was handwritten in pen on the barcode label.

The sergeant picked up the envelope and handed it to her.

"Here you go, Miss Armstrong. The Chief wanted me to let you know we were sorry to have picked you up in this whole mess. We had no idea you were caught up on the street with the demonstrators. He suggested that I urge you, however, to choose your causes more carefully in the future. Associating with people like this can put a permanent black mark on your record if you're not careful."

Cass shook her head. None of this made sense. "The police chief called to bail me out? I don't understand. Why would he do that?"

The sergeant shook his head. "I don't know, Miss. I also don't ask questions when the Chief calls me personally and says to let somebody out of the pen. While I'm at it, hold still and allow me to re-activate your implant.

The sergeant produced the same type of metal tube she'd seen before when they turned off her implant. She wondered once again if there was any risk for permanent damage from having her implant turned on and off like this.

As he held it up next to the implant and pressed the cold metal tube against the side of her face. There was a brief instant of sharp pain inside her head. Then, as if someone turned up the dimmer on a light, she could see again out of her right eye and hear again out of her right ear.

The perpetual fog she'd been operating under for the last few hours lifted, clearing her thoughts as if someone had pulled a heavy blanket off her mind. She smiled, despite the serious nature of the situation.

"Thank you, Sergeant."

"Not a problem. Now let's go ahead and take you out to the front. I'll make sure a car is called for you. I'll have an officer wait by the curb for you until it comes."

Cass started to follow him then stopped. A thought popped into her mind.

The sergeant turned and looked at her. "What's wrong?"

"I can't go," Cass said shaking her head.

"What do you mean, you can't go?"

"I have a friend I was with that got locked up with me. If she can't come with me, then I want you to put me back in the pen."

The sergeant's eyebrows lowered and he scowled at her. "Look, Miss Armstrong, I don't know what got you mixed up with those people in there, but the rest of them will have to make bail on their own. This was serious business. Their little unsanctioned rally turned into a riot."

Cass knew that wasn't what happened but she didn't want to argue with him. She had to think carefully about how she handled this. If she didn't proceed cautiously, the sergeant might throw her from the station and not let her return.

"Sergeant, my friend needs to come with me. I'd hate to have to call your chief and ask him why we weren't both released at the same time. I suspect he'd have to make a second in-person call to you, which he probably wouldn't be happy with."

Cass hoped he didn't call her bluff. She met his eyes and held her gaze level with his.

The sergeant stared at her expressionless for a long time before he said anything, "What's your friend's name?"

"Shelby, Shelby Moore."

"Sit here and don't move. I'll be right back."

Cass sat down in the chair by the sergeant's desk. She placed her hands in her lap and waited.

He turned and walked back towards the rear of the police station toward the holding cells. She could hear him grumbling via her re-enhanced hearing. She couldn't make out the words, but he didn't sound happy.

A few minutes later, the sergeant re-emerged from the back with Shelby in tow. Cass smiled as soon as she spotted her girlfriend. Shelby shot Cass a puzzled glance.

"Shelby, we are getting out of here."

"So I gather," Shelby said.

"Have a seat Miss Moore. I need to reactivate your implants. Once that's done, the two of you, and only the two of you, can be on your way." The sergeant fixed Cass with a stern glance as if daring her to give him another name.

Cass shook her head and the sergeant nodded.

He pulled out the metal tube again and used the device, reactivating Shelby's cerebral implants which also allowed her to move her hand and forearm again.

"That's it, then. You can both come with me towards the front desk. I've called ahead and Miss Moore's personal effects will be waiting for us there."

The pair followed the sergeant through the squad room out to the front lobby of the police station. He walked up to the window and tapped on the glass. Another officer on the far side slid the glass panel back and the sergeant leaned in to say something to him.

The man behind the glass handed another clear envelope to the sergeant. It was just like the one given to Cass earlier. This one had Shelby's name on it along with the barcode and number.

"Here you go, Miss Moore. All of your personal items are in there. Since you're both together, I don't think I need to accompany you to the street and wait for your ride. I have, however, ordered an auto cab for you both. It will be arriving shortly."

"Thank you, Sergeant," Cass said. She smiled at the sergeant. Her mother always told her politeness and kindness went a long way when dealing with people.

The sergeant smiled back then turned and went back through the door into the station.

Shelby whispered to her as they headed outside. "Cass, what the heck is going on? How did you put up my bail?"

"I didn't," Cass explained. "For some reason, the police chief called the sergeant. My name must have popped up when it came through the system. He told the sergeant to let me out. I decided to insist they let you out at the same time or I wasn't going to leave."

"You what?" Shelby exclaimed.

Cass shrugged. "I'm kind of surprised it worked, actually."

Shelby smiled. "Come on, let's go catch that cab before somebody changes their mind."

The two headed down the front steps to the street. While they stood waiting on the curb for the cab to arrive, Shelby looked around. There were other people from the demonstration standing there, probably also waiting for rides.

"I need to call Eric and see how he's doing," Shelby said. "I don't know where he was in the demonstration. Maybe he wasn't picked up by the police."

"It's worth a try," Cass said. "I'm sure a lot of people managed to get away once things got crazy with the police pushing in and arresting people."

Shelby got the blank stare on her face that Cass recognized as her using her implant to do something.

Cass waited for her to finish.

After a few seconds, Shelby shook her head. "He's not answering. It could be he's just off the grid trying to avoid the police. It could also mean he's back in that station under arrest with all the men in another cell."

"I'm not sure I can go back in there and demand a third person get released," Cass said. "You heard what he said."

"Let's worry about where he is after we get back to the campus. He's probably fine and just hiding out. I left a message via text on his system. When he checks back in, he'll get it."

An auto cab pulled up. Cass spotted "Armstrong" scrolling across the windshield of the vehicle. She pointed. "There's our car."

The two jumped in the back of the cab while Cass gave the university address to the AI driver. She sat back and looked over her shoulder as the police station faded into the distance.

Cass knew Shelby worried about her brother, no matter how much she tried to put on a brave face. Cass needed to help her find out where he was. They could both dig into that once they were safely back at school.

Chapter 22

THE NEXT DAY, Cass found it challenging to pay attention to her studies. She had several assignments due, but she couldn't concentrate because Shelby paced the room behind her.

She had tried contacting her brother at least once every hour since they'd returned the day before. There was no word from him at all.

"Shel, you need to relax. He's fine. I'm sure of it. If there were something major wrong, you'd have heard from the hospital or something. Maybe he's still in police custody and they aren't letting him make bail yet. I think they have 48 hours to do that."

"This isn't some police holovid, Cass. This is real life. My brother has disappeared. And nobody knows where he is and no vid show detective is going to show up and help us find him."

"You contacted all the hospitals. He hasn't turned up in any of them. He's either still hiding out for some reason and can't contact you, or he's in police custody. Either way, he's safe."

Shelby started to say something then stopped. "I know I'm driving you nuts. I just feel so helpless being here and not being able to do anything."

"Why don't you try to concentrate on some of your class work. You don't want to get behind. Finals are in only a few weeks."

Shelby went over and sat down at her desk. "I'll try. But I'm so distracted thinking about Eric."

Cass nodded. "That's completely understandable. Try to dig into your work. Pick one thing to do and take your mind off of thinking about it for a while."

A few minutes later, Cass checked on Shelby. It seemed to be working. At least she'd stopped pacing the room and sat down to work.

Cass's advice and constant support helped Shelby get through the next two worrisome days. That was how long it took for her to get word of Eric's whereabouts.

Cass came out of her second class Tuesday morning when a voice message pinged her system from Shelby. "They found him. He's in police custody. He finally reached out to Mom and Dad to arrange his bail."

Cass listened to the voice message playing over her implant's internal system then called her girlfriend.

Shelby picked up right away. "Cass, Mom and Dad need us to go down and bail out Eric. Dad wired me the money. Something's going on with them and they can't travel here without getting into some sort of trouble themselves. They're under police investigation, too, because of their association with Eric."

"How can the police bring them in on this?" Cass asked. "They had nothing to do with the demonstration. They weren't even in the same state."

"I don't know. Somehow, they're putting pressure on him through them."

"All right, I'll go down with you to the police station. I assume he's at the central booking area where we were before."

"Yes, I think so. I'll meet you back at the room. I'm headed there now."

Cass picked up her pace heading across campus. She figured, based upon where her classes were, that she'd beat Shelby back to the room. She was surprised to find Shelby there ahead of her.

"How did you get here so quickly?"

"I ran all the way here. I wanted to make sure I was here when you got here. We need to go right away. I don't want Eric to spend one more minute in that jail cell."

Shelby headed out the door and Cass followed her, pulling the door shut behind her.

"Shel, slow down a little bit. He's fine. We finally found him."

"You and I were upset about being in jail and we were only in the cell for a few hours. How do you think he must feel?"

Cass reached out over the Mantle as they left the dorm and called for an auto cab to meet them out front. When they walked down to the curb, it pulled up.

"There's our ride," Cass said. "Come on. We'll head downtown and get Eric right now."

The two girls got in the auto cab and sat back while it drove them down to the police station. They were not prepared for what they saw when they arrived.

"What the hell is going on here?" Shelby asked as they got out of the cab.

There were people lined up all around the police station. Some sort of demonstration was going on and Cass couldn't figure out what it was.

Then, she heard it.

"No subs, not here! No subs, not here!"

The crowd's chant was one she'd heard before. Her father had once called it the Sapiens battle cry. The words labeled the people here outside the police station as Sapiens sympathizers if not actual movement members.

The chants washed over Cass and Shelby as the two of them stood alone at the curb while the cab pulled away into traffic.

"No subs, not here! No subs, not here!"

"Shel, someone must've let them know prisoners from the cyber-rights demonstration are being held here."

"We can't bring Eric out into this mob."

"I agree," Cass said. "We should try to find another way into the police station. It's a bad idea for us to push our way through this crowd."

The shouts grew louder around them. People still hadn't noticed the two of them standing at the back of the group.

Shelby grabbed Cass's hand and shook her head. "I'm going in there. You don't have to come with me if you don't want to, but I have to go in and get Eric out."

Cass studied the angry crowd. No one was looking in their direction right now, but she had a feeling that this particular group of people would spot their implants right away if the two of them weren't careful.

"Shel, let's be careful," Cass said, leaning in so Shelby could hear her over the shouting. "Stay close together and keep your head down. Let's try not to jostle anybody and draw attention to ourselves."

Shelby nodded and together, hand-in-hand, they worked their way forward to the front steps of the police station. About halfway through the crowd, someone noticed them. With every step the pair took, more people around them turned and directed their shouts at them, yelling into their faces as they pushed and jostled the two women.

"You're not human. Go home."

"Get out of here, sub. You're not wanted around here."

Shelby and Cass kept their mouths shut and continued to press forward. The crowd let them through, but not without jostling them some as they passed by.

The two of them finally made it to the steps of the police station. The shouts and screams of the crowd grew louder as they moved into the open and were spotted by others in the mob who hadn't seen them yet.

"Come on," Cass called out over the wash of angry sound. "We need to get inside before the crowd decides to do more than shout at us."

Together, the two raced up the steps, bursting into the lobby of the police station.

There was no one else inside but a desk sergeant on the other side of the glass window. Shelby walked up to him and waited while the female sergeant slid the glass window to one side.

"Yes, miss?" The sergeant asked. She didn't stand up to talk with them, remaining on her stool and eyeing them with a bored glance up from her computer screen.

Shelby leaned on the counter. "I'm here to pick up Eric Moore. I have his bail money."

The sergeant tapped a few things on a keypad while she stared at the screen in front of her. After a moment, the woman nodded and looked up at Shelby.

"He's in custody at the prison ward at County General."

"The hospital?" Shelby asked. "What's he doing in the hospital?"

The sergeant shrugged. "It just says that's where he is. You still pay his bail here and I'll give you a ticket to go pick him up."

Shelby grunted and took her credit ID out, handing it over to the officer. "The money is all there. You can take it from that account."

The sergeant took the credit ID chip and ran it through the system. She handed it back to Shelby after a few seconds and then gave her a hard copy of the release paperwork.

"I've also attached the receipt to your credit ID should you lose the paperwork."

Shelby folded the paper and slid it into her jeans pocket and then put the credit ID back in her other pocket. She turned to leave, but Cass put a hand on her shoulder to stop her. She pointed at the crowd outside. They could hear the hate-filled chants here inside the police station lobby.

"Why don't I find another way out of the building for you two," the desk sergeant said. "There's no need for you both to leave through that mess out front."

"Thank you," Cass said. "We appreciate that."

The sergeant smiled and said, "Wait there, I'll have an officer lead you out through the squad entrance. You'll be able to walk up the ramp from the parking garage to the street beside the station. That should take you out where there are no protesters."

"Thank you," Cass said.

True to her word, a few minutes later, an officer appeared to escort Shelby and Cass through the police station. They went down a long hallway to a stairwell, following it down to an underground garage.

Police vehicles lined the spaces on either side of them as the officer led them through the garage. He stopped at the exit ramp up to the street.

"You can go out that way." He stopped at the bottom and watched as the two girls kept going. There were no signs of any protesters at the top, although the sounds of their chanting and shouts reached them from the front of the station.

"Come on Cass, we have to get to the hospital. I don't understand why they didn't report him as being there when I contacted them before. There's nothing in this paperwork that explains what is wrong with him."

"He was in police custody," Cass said. "Maybe the hospital records didn't show him as being there because it's in a different system."

Shelby had already called ahead for an auto cab. They waited a few minutes, watching the sidewalk leading to the front of the building for any sign of protesters heading their way.

The cab soon pulled up and they jumped in. The vehicle pulled away from the police station and headed across town to County General Hospital. Cass wondered how Eric had gotten injured as they went. The people in with Shelby and her in the jail had nothing worse than bumps and bruises.

At the hospital, Cass and Shelby walked into the main lobby, unsure where to go and ask about Eric.

Cass pointed to an elderly woman with a name tag sitting behind a counter ahead of them.

Shelby walked up to the woman sitting there. "Excuse me, I'm looking for my brother, Eric Moore?"

"Just a moment, dearie. while I check the database."

The woman accessed a tablet on the desktop and tapped in a few commands. She looked up after a second and said, "I don't have anyone here registered under that name. Are you sure he's a patient at the hospital?"

"Yes, he's here. We just came from the police station. He's in police custody or something like that?"

"Oh, why didn't you say so? I don't have that information here in this database. I'll contact someone who can help you."

Shelby took a step back while the woman contacted someone over the local comm system. Cass put an arm around Shelby's waist, pulling her close.

"It's going to be all right Shel. I'm sure he's fine. He might have gotten a little roughed up by the police, but they have good doctors here. They took good care of him."

"I hope so. Eric likes to put on a façade, but he's not as tough as he thinks he is. I'm afraid he said or did something that made the police angry when he was arrested."

"Let's not worry about that right now. Look, here comes someone." Cass indicated a man in a police uniform walking across the lobby from a bank of elevators.

"I understand you two ladies are here to see a prisoner?" The police officer asked as he walked over.

"Yes," Shelby began. She fished in her pocket and pulled out the receipt from posting bail. "We're here to pick him up. We posted his bail at the central district police station."

The officer reached out for the paper. He read it over before handing it back to Shelby.

"Wait right here. I'll have him escorted down to you."

The police officer left, heading back towards the elevators.

Cass turned to Shelby. "See, that wasn't so bad, was it? Eric will be here before you know it."

Shelby returned her smile.

Cass liked what she saw in that grin. There was a glimmer of hope in her eyes for the first time in days.

It took almost fifteen minutes for them to bring Eric down to the lobby. Cass saw him first and couldn't contain her horror as she gasped out loud when she spotted him.

He looked awful.

The bruises all around his face and head gave him a puffy, swollen appearance. His arm was in a sling and he rode in a wheelchair pushed by a hospital orderly. The police officer walked behind them.

Shelby heard Cass's gasp and turned around. As soon as she saw him, she ran to her brother.

"Eric," Shelby called out. "What did they do to you? You bastards will pay for this."

"Shelby, calm down," Eric said through swollen, cracked lips. "You're going to get yourself arrested if you're not careful."

Eric had trouble with some of the words. It was clear his mouth had something wrong with it. He didn't open it. Instead, he talked through gritted teeth.

"Eric, what's wrong with your mouth?" Shelby asked.

"Broken jaw," he said in a raspy voice. "The doctors had to wire it shut. It's one of the reasons I'm here in the hospital."

"Miss," the orderly asked. "The police officer said I'm to turn him over to you. But we should probably put him in a vehicle directly from the wheelchair. He's not really up to walking right now."

Shelby glared at the police officer standing behind the wheelchair. He responded with a grin.

Cass pulled Shelby away from a possible confrontation with the cop so they could follow the orderly pushing Eric towards the doors outside. As they drew close, Eric reached out to hold Shelby's hand in his.

"I'll call and order a cab," Cass said. She accessed her comm system and called up an auto cab for them outside of the hospital. They waited with the orderly in silence for the five minutes it took the vehicle to show up.

The orderly helped them move Eric into the front passenger seat then smiled and wished them well. He walked away with the wheelchair, leaving them alone on the sidewalk in front of the hospital.

"Let's just go home, Shel," Eric said. "I'm tired and I want to sleep in my own bed for a change."

"Eric, we have to do something about what they did to you. We have to tell someone and take them to court or something."

Eric shook his head. "We'll talk about it in the morning. Right now, I just want to go home and get some rest."

As if to punctuate his statement, Eric laid his head over to the side against the seatbelt restraint running up from his shoulder and closed his eyes.

Cass reached out and gripped Shelby's hand, her fingers between Shel's and holding it tight. She smiled, trying to reassure her girlfriend as the car drove them back across the city towards Eric's apartment.

Chapter 23

ERIC'S APARTMENT was small and surprisingly neat considering a guy lived there. "If I didn't know better, Eric," Cass said to lighten the mood, "I'd think you had a maid or something. Are you sure your mother doesn't come by and pick up after you?"

Eric groaned. "I just don't like things that are a mess."

"Which is why you're going to let us hang here for a couple of days and help get you squared away, big brother," Shelby said. "You look awful and there's no way you're going to be able to do any shopping or take care of yourself while your arm is in a sling and you can barely walk."

"I'll be all right, Sis. Really, I will. The docs gave me a dose of quick heal. I'll feel better soon. I just need some rest, that's all."

"Well, let's get you in your bed and we'll talk about it again when you wake up," Shelby said. She nodded to Cass and the two of them held him under his arms as he walked on unsteady legs towards the bedroom. They got him tucked into bed and came back out to the living room.

Shelby leaned close to Cass and said in a low voice, "One of us needs to go down to the corner store and pick up some groceries.

His jaw is wired shut, so I assume he's going to have to have his food mashed up in some way so he can actually eat it."

"We passed that diner on the way here," Cass said. "It's only a few blocks away. I'll bet they have something like milkshakes there. They probably have mashed potatoes, too. We could probably get those for him to start and then figure out the rest later on."

Shelby nodded. "Good idea. While you're out doing that, I'll do a search of the net and figure out exactly how we're supposed to take care of him while he heals up."

Cass hugged Shelby and then turned and left the apartment. She rode the elevator down to the ground floor and headed out to the street. It was time to get some shopping in.

She didn't know what Eric liked, but she figured she could at least pick up the basics. Cass started a list using her implant as she walked towards the corner market. She'd stop there first and then hit the diner afterward.

Cass and Shelby ended up staying with Eric for three days. They both got permission from their professors to miss class and work remotely. It wasn't a big deal since they'd already turned in most of their assignments for the end of the year via the school's net connection.

Once they had their school work squared away, it gave them a chance to help Eric embark on the road to recovery. He was much steadier on his feet the day after they got home and he improved a great deal every day until he was pretty much back to normal on the third day except for his broken jaw. He still had to eat all his food by way of a straw.

At the end of the day on Thursday, Eric convinced them to return to the dorm.

Cass remarked as they headed to the door, "Hopefully you can get some rest through the weekend. We'll check back in with you then."

"You're not coming to the rally?" Eric asked.

Cass shot him a look then glanced at Shelby. They both thought this discussion had been settled.

Shelby took the lead after a nod from Cass. "Bro, you're not going to any rally this weekend. Let the Sapiens have their stupid event. You don't need to show up and prove anything to anyone. Stay home and get better. There'll be other rallies and demonstrations to go to."

Eric shook his head. "No. My injuries make it that much more important for me to be there. I have to prove to the police, the Sapiens goons, and everyone else, we will stand up for ourselves. We're not going to be deterred by their treatment of us. Just because there are a few bigots in the police department, doesn't mean all of them are that way. Most of them treated me well. I have to trust that someone will stand up for us at some point."

"It's a problem if the Chief of Police is one of those bigoted police officers," Cass said.

"What do you mean?" Shelby asked. "How could you possibly know that?"

"Think, Shelby. It was the police chief who saw my name and called the station to have me let go. My father mentioned meeting with him. He's obviously a friend of my father. The two of them met regarding the Sapiens' march this weekend. He's a sympathizer at the very least."

"And you think this means the chief is part of the Sapiens Movement?" Eric asked.

Cass nodded. "My father met with him and some of the other leaders in the city. I know they talked about the upcoming rally. The police chief may not be an active member of the party. He is helping facilitate the rally for my father, whatever his motivations. I think we have to accept that the officers assigned to the Saturday march will be friendly to the movement and not to any cyber-human countermarch."

Eric sat still in his chair for several seconds. Shelby and Cass waited for him to say something. Hopefully, he'd change his mind.

When he looked up at them, Cass knew he hadn't. His determined expression made him almost look fierce.

"It doesn't change anything. I overheard a few of the officers talking about how the Sapiens march was providing all their own security. Only a minimal police presence was needed. That means those people will have the run of our city if we don't stand up to them. If we back down, we let them win. We can't do that. I'm still going to the rally and countermarch on Saturday."

"Then we're going with you," Shelby said.

"Shel?" Cass asked. "It's going to be dangerous. I'm not sure we'll be so lucky again."

"Cass, we have to go, especially if you have some connection within the police that might help us. You might be able to use the chief to swing some sort of safeguard if we need it at the last minute."

"I don't think it works that way," Cass said. "I don't even know the chief's name."

"Cass," Shelby implored her. "We have to go. Eric is in no condition to go alone."

Cass paused. None of this seemed like a good idea. She still nodded because she knew both Shelby and her brother would go without her if she refused.

Shelby smiled at her and turned to Eric. "That settles it. We're going with you. When do you plan on leaving Saturday morning?"

Eric smiled. "I'm glad you're with me. We need to reach out and find out how many others from the original organizing committee got out of jail. Everyone should've made bail by now. Once we know that, we can gather them together and make plans for what to do on Saturday."

"Cass and I will help with that. We should be able to track down everybody if you give us the list of names. You stay here and focus on getting better. We'll do the legwork for you in the meantime."

Eric hesitated before answering. "All right. If you ladies insist, I'll let you do it."

Shelby leaned over and hugged her brother in the chair and then walked with Cass towards the door. The two of them left the apartment and headed for the elevator.

"Shelby, I still think this is a bad idea."

"I do, too, but what else am I supposed to do? I can't lock him in his apartment and he will still find a way to get there whether we take him or not."

"So, we're just going to let him get arrested again? You know that's what's going to happen if there's another counter-march. Given how weak he is, that wouldn't be a good outcome. I'm also afraid what the Sapiens marchers will do when directly confronted with a group of cyber-human protesters."

"You think they'll get violent?" Shelby asked. "The police will be there to keep the groups apart."

"You heard what Eric said. The movement is providing their own security for the march. There may not be enough police to keep the two groups apart. The streets are going to be filled with people holding strong opposing views. A lot of the Sapiens marchers will think there's a genuine, physical danger from people who have cybernetic enhancements. They'll believe we can do everything from reading minds to pulling out weapons hidden in prosthetic limbs like your arm."

"That's ridiculous. This is a normal hand except for the fact that it has some extra capabilities."

"It's those capabilities, those extras, that people are most afraid of. They don't understand or know that for you it's just like carrying a penknife."

Shelby was silent for the rest of the ride down the elevator. A signal pinged their implants as they left the apartment building. Eric sent them the list of people to contact.

"Looks like everybody on this list is not too far away from here. We should be able to connect with them either via the net or visit their home or apartment directly," Cass said.

"Agreed. Let's start with the top of the list and work our way down. We'll send out a message to them first using the contact info Eric provided us. If we don't hear back from them, we'll stop and try to visit them in person."

Cass and Shelby started working their way down the list of all the people who'd been in jail. All of them had made bail and were either safe at home or back to work. The group agreed to come to

Eric's apartment Saturday morning and meet with him to determine how they were going to proceed.

Cass and Shelby headed back to their dorm to pick up some clothes before going back to Eric's apartment. He was doing better, but since he wanted to attend the rally, Shelby wanted to stay there through the weekend so they could be close to him the whole time.

Chapter 24

SATURDAY ARRIVED TOO QUICKLY. Cass woke that morning with a start, jolted from a horrible dream by her internal alarm. Though she couldn't remember the details of the nightmare, it left her with a sense of dread she couldn't shake.

On several occasions that morning, as she, Shelby, and Eric had an early breakfast around his kitchen table, she considered telling the two of them about her feelings. Eric's infectious enthusiasm and talk about how they were going to make a real difference later that morning changed her mind. Cass pressed the dread down deep within herself until she could barely feel it anymore.

Shelby must have sensed her mood anyway because when Eric went back to his room to change for the rally, she reached across the small kitchen table and laid a hand on Cass's arm.

"What's wrong? You've been brooding about something all morning."

"It's nothing. I woke up with a bad feeling about today. That's all. It's probably just a combination of bad dreams and the memory of last Saturday."

"We're going to be more careful this time around. You and I are just there to keep an eye on Eric. We'll keep to the sidelines and make sure we have a way out if things turn nasty again."

"I hope that's good enough, Shel. You don't know the members of the movement the way I do. They are true believers, some of them rabidly so."

"You used to be one of them. If you can change your mind about us, so can they. We have to show them who we are and that we're not a threat to them. Eric and his friends will be peaceful."

"We were peaceful last weekend and look where that got us," Cass remarked.

Shelby didn't answer right away. After a few seconds she said, "Look, Cass, you don't have to come today if you don't want to. I've got to go because Eric's not going to stay here and someone needs to go and keep him from doing anything rash. I know him. He feels like he needs to show his friends that he's stronger than a few heavy-handed police officers. I'm afraid, like you, even with peaceful intent, the Sapiens marchers are going to precipitate something against Eric and the others."

"If you agree with me, Shel, why are we going along with him on this march today? You have to do something to keep him here."

"If I do that, he'll just kick us out and then go down there on his own. No. We need to follow through with what we started helping to organize today's rally. If we are there with him, we can keep him out of trouble."

Cass didn't answer. There was no need. Shelby had made up her mind. Cass's only options were to go along or go home.

Eric returned from getting dressed and grabbed his coat. "You ladies ready to go?"

Cass glanced at Shelby and nodded. Shelby smiled back at her and got up from the chair in the kitchen. "Let me grab my coat."

As Cass grabbed her own coat, her girlfriend leaned over and whispered, "Thank you, my love."

The three of them left and headed to the rally point for the cyber-rights supporters. It was time to see if they could change some minds. Cass knew most were likely to be intractable.

As soon as they reached the streets close to City Hall, it was clear the Sapiens event was much larger than any of them had expected it to be. Everywhere they looked, there were people wearing T-shirts with some pretty offensive slogans on them, all aimed against cyber-humans.

Many were quite shocking. One had the image of a bullseye target and the words, "The Only Good Sub Is A Dead Sub."

Cass had never seen such blatant hatred displayed before, even growing up within the Sapiens enclave. If frightened her and she was unprepared for the visceral anger she felt at seeing it here.

Cass realized how much her father had sheltered her from. There was no way he was unaware of this element in the Sapiens movement while she was growing up. That meant he hid it from her and Elena.

The three of them avoided contact with the people walking towards the Sapiens rally, instead heading straight for another smaller park near City Hall where Eric had told the counter-marchers to meet.

The other demonstrators for the cyber-humans were waiting in the park when they arrived. The number of supporters surprised Cass given what happened the week before. There weren't the thousand or so from the previous week, but several hundred people still decided to brave the trials of a counter-protest again this weekend. All of them carried signs and placards, ready to go.

Eric walked around to the front of the group and climbed up on a bench. He winced a little as he stood up above the assembled people. He was still sore from his injuries the previous weekend.

Someone handed Eric a bull horn and he began to pass along instructions to the group. Cass and Shelby stood off to one side as he addressed the supporters in the park.

"Fellow cyber-humans, this is our chance to stand up for who we are and what we believe in. We are not going to let them bully us or back down from their hatred. Now is our chance to stand up to evil. We have to show them they can't drive us underground."

A cheer went up from the group as people raised their fists over their heads and waved the signs they held in the air.

"Follow me, be peaceful, and march for freedom and basic rights for everyone." Eric stepped down from the park bench and started towards the street.

The rest of the group moved forward, following behind him, chanting out the slogan, "Cyber Rights, Right Now."

Cass and Shelby held back a little and situated themselves at the periphery of the group.

All of them marched forward onto the street, turning right towards the square in front of City Hall where the Sapiens rally was being held.

Stragglers still filtering into the Sapiens rally called out a few slurs at them but they encountered no organized resistance.

Cass knew that couldn't last for too long. She looked around, searching for an escape plan. Her feeling of dread from the previous night's horrific dream had returned.

About a block from City Hall, Cass noticed an alley off to their left with a fire escape hanging down on the side of one of the buildings. That might be a way up to higher ground if they lost sight of Eric.

This week, unlike the previous weekend, there was almost zero police presence on the streets around the square. Cass did spot numerous men and women in yellow windbreakers with "SAPIENS SECURITY" stenciled on the back. Clearly, her father's plan to provide their own security for the event had been embraced by the police chief and mayor.

As the cyber-human demonstrators turned the corner and started up the street towards City Hall, they ran into the first large group of Sapiens demonstrators almost immediately.

The Sapiens' attendees in this group all wore black sweaters and sweatshirts with a stylized fist inside a white circle printed on them. Cass had never seen the logo before.

The black-clad group turned to face them as the cyber-human group approached.

Between the two approaching groups, stood a thin line of people wearing the yellow security jackets, spaced about five feet apart. There were no more than a dozen of them. Even if they were inclined to keep the two groups apart, which Cass wasn't sure they were, there was no way they'd stop a confrontation from happening.

Before Cass knew it, both groups surged towards each other, shouting angry threats and curses.

She wasn't sure who charged first. In the end, it didn't matter.

The groups pressed together and fighting erupted between those standing in the front of both groups.

Cass and Shelby lost sight of Eric as soon as the groups converged.

"Cass, can you see Eric?" Shelby asked, panic in her voice.

She craned her neck, trying to pick Eric out of the melee in front of them. Cass shook her head. "No, can you?"

Shelby shook her head, too. "What are we going to do?"

Cass remembered the alley they'd passed a hundred feet behind them. "I saw an alley over there. I think we might be able to better see what's going on if we get up on the roof of that building."

"How are we going to help Eric from up there?"

"I don't think we are in a position to help Eric at all now, no matter what happens, Shel. You and I aren't fighters. We aren't going to be able to wade in there and pull him out of that melee. All we'd do is end up getting hurt ourselves. That won't help Eric."

Cass hooked a thumb over her shoulder. "Maybe, though, we can see where Eric is from up there. If we can spot him, we can track his location to meet up with him later. At the very least, we'll see if he gets picked up by police."

"What police? We haven't seen any for several blocks."

Cass glanced behind them and shook her head. "There's got to be more police officers nearby somewhere. Don't worry. They'll break up this fight soon enough and lock up everyone, just like last week, including those Sapiens goons."

Shelby looked doubtful but nodded. Cass grabbed her by the hand and together they ran half a block to the rear of the surging group of cyber-human demonstrators and turned down an alley to the left. Cass pointed to the fire escape. The stairs at the bottom had already been lowered to near ground level. Together, she and Shelby climbed up the black metal staircase to the roof of the five-story apartment building.

By the time they got to the rooftop and reached the front edge of the building to scan the street below, things had gotten much worse on the ground. From the center of the group of Sapiens supporters came another black-clad group of men and women wearing the same logo with the fist emblazoned on it. They wore ski masks pulled down over their faces.

The newcomers all carried baseball bats and other improvised weapons. They pushed to the front of the group where the fighting was thickest, wading in to start beating on the cyber-humans shoving forward from the other direction. Above it all, with eerie clarity, Cass could hear the voices of the Sapiens' rally speakers coming from the stage a hundred yards away in front of City Hall. She had a clear view of the stage from her vantage point.

The current speaker on the stage said similar things to those said by her parents around the dinner table as she grew up.

The woman speaking at the moment called out to the crowd. "Are you tired of all the traditions of decency and justice being trampled by those who want to take away our freedom? They talk about the freedom of rights granted to all humans when they aren't human anymore themselves."

The crowd cheered in response and she continued. "That's laughable because these people willingly gave up their humanity to become machines. We know what happens to machines that don't do what we want them to do, don't we?"

"Junk them," many in the crowd shouted, eliciting a shout and laughter from the woman on stage.

"It is they who threaten us," the woman continued. "They're readying themselves for the time when they'll use their superior strength and power to vanquish all of us and make us all just like them."

Cass was struck by the contrast between what the woman said and the vicious violence being perpetrated by the so-called pure humans on the cyber-enhanced people protesting below.

The cyber-human demonstrators retreated, falling back in an

attempt to get away from the surge of the black-clad masked thugs who'd come out from the center of the Sapiens group. Then, in an instant, the cyber-humans below broke up into clusters of two and three people, dropping their signs and banners as they turned and ran from the brutal attackers in front of them. None of them were prepared to face this kind of opposition.

The street below cleared out, leaving numerous people lying on the ground, bloody and injured.

"Cass, you have the ocular implant. Where's Eric?"

Cass scanned the group of those who were retreating, hoping to catch a glimpse of Eric among those fleeing from the fight. She didn't see him anywhere.

Cass shook her head. "I don't see him in the group that's fleeing. He must be still up at the front with the few that are still fighting."

Shelby groaned beside her. This was more evil than their worst fears.

Cass shifted to scan the area where there were knots of struggling people from both groups. After a few seconds, she spotted Eric and a half dozen others.

A group of about a dozen masked protesters had them in custody along with a small group of the yellow-jacketed security guards. Their captors dragged Eric and the others into the crowded square, disappearing into the crowd before they were blocked by a line of trees. They all looked like they'd taken a pretty severe beating.

Cass pointed as she clutched Shelby's shoulder. "There. I saw him with some others from our rally being pulled back into the Sapiens' crowd."

"What the hell are they going to do with him?" Shelby asked. "They certainly aren't going to let him speak."

Cass shrugged. "Some of those with him had those yellow security coats on. Maybe they're taking them to a police checkpoint for arrest?"

She wasn't sure that was accurate but what else could they be doing with them other than letting them go? Cass couldn't come up with a definite answer, so she offered up the only suggestion she could think of.

"Maybe they're helping them to a first aid station."

"That's bull, Cass. Those people were the ones that beat them. They're not going to help them get first aid."

Cass spotted them again on the other side of the cluster of trees. They were much closer to the stage now. She used her telephoto ocular function to follow the group as they were dragged forward.

Her implant automatically recorded everything she saw on a looped recording chip. It constantly updated with the most recent two hours of visual images and sound picked up by her ocular and auditory implants.

It was a fun thing to have when coming and going from lectures since she could share and save files remotely via the Mantle.

Now, however, her recording documented horrible things. Cass wasn't sure she wanted to keep any of this video, though she knew she probably had to. If anything happened to Eric and the others, they'd need evidence of what she saw below.

"Cass, we have to get down there. We have to do something to get Eric out of there."

"We can't go down there Shel. They'll just pull us into the middle of their rally and beat us up, too. You call the police. I don't know why there aren't any around. I'll continue to follow Eric and the others through the crowd. I can still see them from up here. I'll send you the video feed over the Mantle so you can see what I'm seeing."

Shelby nodded and concentrated as she started to place the call over her implant. Cass sent her girlfriend the link to the video feed while she listened.

"Hello, 911? I am at the Sapiens demonstration downtown. From where I'm standing, I can see several cyber-humans being beaten and dragged away by members of the rally. You need to send help to them. They're being dragged towards City Hall and the stage erected there."

Shelby went silent for a few seconds as she listened to the dispatcher respond on the other end. "No, you don't understand. I think something awful is going to happen to them. They're injured and need medical attention."

Shelby paused again. "But I don't see any police. That's why I'm calling you. How can you tell me there're plenty of police officers there when I don't see any around?"

Another pause, then Shelby continued her plea, desperation causing her voice to crack, "You need to send more. I'm telling you, there aren't enough. You have to stop this."

Shelby went silent again and shook her head. She apparently wasn't getting the response she wanted from the city's emergency center. Her shoulders sagged and she shook her head one last time.

"She hung up on me. She told me they were doing all they can do and I had to clear the line for people with real emergencies. How could she do that to me?"

Cass didn't know what to say. She wanted to turn and hug Shelby but she couldn't lose sight of Eric and the others. She held her focus on the events going on over in the square.

Cass tried to comfort her girlfriend as she lost Eric in the crowd again. "Shel, we can't go down there and do anything. I've lost sight of him. Let's stay up here and see if we can find out where they took your brother. Then we can try again to get some help for him."

The two of them scanned the crowded square below and tried to catch a glimpse of Eric.

Chapter 25

THE STREET directly below them was now empty of anyone other than Sapiens demonstrators. The counter-demonstration had broken up and the people who could had run away. A small group of police officers finally arrived and gathered up the few wounded from both sides, clustering them on the sidewalk and tending to them with a few EMTs from an ambulance parked on the curb across the street from their perch.

Cass pointed to what the police were doing. "See, Shelby, the police are here taking charge and protecting the remaining people from the fight. That's a good sign."

Shelby didn't even look. She continued to watch the square, trying to spot her brother. Cass recorded video of the police here treating some of the injured. She captured it all on her implant.

"Cass, what are we going to do?" Shelby asked. Cass heard the desperation in her girlfriend's voice.

"If we leave now, we take a chance of getting roughed up by the crowd below. Even with those few officers down there, the safest place for us is up here."

Cass turned and scanned the main crowd again. She had a clear view of the entire stage area and most of the rest of the square except for a few places where trees blocked her line of sight. The crowd in support of the Sapiens rally was bigger than she'd expected.

A small part of her mind wondered if her father was monitoring the size of the rally from home. He would be proud of what they'd accomplished here, as awful as it was from Cass's standpoint.

Activity near the stage area caught her attention. She zoomed in on the platform. The person currently speaking finished their talk. As they left the stage, music played and there was some evidence that another speaker was getting ready to make their entrance. The song was a current pop hit and the crowd sang along with the peppy tune.

Cass searched the area around the stage. Eric had been pulled in that direction minutes before. Perhaps he'd been taken there. She scanned the side of the stage as the new speaker started his presentation.

The man's words sent a chill down Cass's spine and she shifted her view to the center of the stage. A man stood in front of the microphone wearing a black ski mask and a black t-shirt with the circled fist logo on it. He had a standard ink tattoo of the same black fist logo on his left forearm.

"People of the Sapiens movement, look up here and see what humanity might become if we're not careful."

Cass broadened her view of the stage area and stiffened. Eric and six others were standing on the stage in a line behind the man who spoke. A pair of the masked thugs held each of them.

"This is what will allow the machines to take over. This is what will allow the Mantle to rule us. Some say it's inevitable. We say it is not. We are your first line of defense. We, the members of Sapiens First will defend your rights and your families."

Cass had told Shelby that the radical Sapiens First faction of the movement was a myth. She'd thought it was correct at the time. She now knew how wrong she was.

"Shelby, I see Eric."

"Where? I dropped your feed. Is he all right?"

"He looks a little beaten up and bloody but he is alive. They have him along with six others up on the stage."

Shelby gasped and leaned forward over the edge of the building to try and see better.

Cass tried to reassure her. "As long as he's up there, the rest of the crowd can't get to them. That's a good thing. It looks like they're just holding Eric and the others up as an example of what they hate. It's not pretty, but he's safe for now."

"Cass, how are we going to get them down from there?"

"I don't think we want to right now. That crowd is pretty worked up. They're out for blood. I'm sure they'd like nothing more than to beat up on people like Eric and us."

"But how is he going to get out of there?"

"I don't know. But as long as he's up on that stage right in front of City Hall, it's probably the safest place he can be."

The man on the stage continued speaking to the crowd. "A lot of you people ask, what can you do? A lot of you people ask, is a political movement enough? Well, I have the answer for you. No, a political movement is not enough. We have to fight back. We have to stand up for humanity because if we don't, no one else will."

The crowd cheered in response and shouted at the stage and a chill ran down Cass's spine. She'd never seen this side of the Sapiens movement before. It had always been peaceful in her community. People talked about trying to keep their families safe. No one talked about doing so with violence or unrest.

"We, as Sapiens First," the man on stage continued. "We, the ones who stand ready to defend your lives and your families, are hereby serving a notice to the subs who say all they want is to live peacefully among us. We don't believe their lies and we're not going to let them pretend they're just like us. We are not going to allow it anymore."

The speaker pulled the wireless microphone from the stand and walked along the line of prisoners. Cass zoomed in. Eric stood in the middle of the group of seven. He looked dazed, trying to comprehend what was going on.

"Cass, I can't see what's going on down there. What's happening? I can see the stage, but everything looks so small."

"Stop trying to see it with your eyes. I'm streaming it to you. I can see everything. Open your tablet and load the stream there if you want."

Shelby pulled out her tablet from the purse on her shoulder and activated it.

A few seconds later Cass approved the connection between the device and her implant.

Shelby gasped as a close-up image of Eric and the others on the stage came into focus on her screen.

"Oh my God, Cass. He looks awful."

"Yes, but he's alive. That's all that matters. If we can see him, so can the police and everyone else."

"I'm going to stream this to the net via the Mantle. This has to go out to spread the word of what is happening here. We need to show what animals these Sapiens First bastards are."

Cass had a momentary stab of fear. "Shel, this video can't come from me. I can't be the one who recorded this."

"Don't worry, I'm sending it from my device. It'll go out anonymously. There'll be no connection to you. As far as anyone will know, I'm streaming this from a standard webcam."

Cass kept her face turned towards the stage, holding the magnified image in the frame as she watched what happened below.

The man walked back down the line of captives on stage. He'd continued ranting about the threat of the Mantle AI and its desire to take over of humanity. Cass had stopped listening to his words because he kept repeating himself.

Then he said something that drew her attention again. The man said something about a "final solution" and the "end game." The words sounded ominous.

"People of the Sapiens movement, it is time for you to witness what must be the one and only final solution to this problem. The only way we can defend ourselves from what is to come is to eliminate it before it's too late. We must begin the end game now."

Some of this sounded strangely familiar to Cass. She'd heard it before. Her father and mother had talked about something they called the end game.

When she first heard it from them, she thought it was some sort of final political plan to get Sapiens members into the Congress or something. Coming from the masked leader on stage, it sounded much worse.

A hush fell over the crowd as the speaker paused with his hand held out in front of him. There seemed to be a sense of anticipation as everyone watched, their eyes riveted to the stage. The masked man reached down to his belt and pulled up a round metal tube.

It looked familiar. It took a second for Cass to place where she'd seen it before. Then it hit her. It was a device like the one the police used to disable implants on people in custody. This one was different. It had a coiled cord extending from it to a pouch on the man's belt, like a battery pack. He spread his arms, holding the tube over his head. The coiled cord stretched up along his arm.

"Are you ready for the end game?"

The crowd responded with scattered cheers from various places across the square. The majority of the attendees seemed as confused as Cass was about what the man intended to do.

The masked speaker put his hand to his ear and said, "That didn't sound very encouraging. I ask you again, are you ready for the end game?"

This time the cheers reverberated as more people joined in.

"I'm only going to ask one more time. Are you ready for us to begin the end game?"

This time the entire crowd erupted in cheers and shouts of encouragement.

Cass struggled to understand what was happening. What was the end game? She scanned back-and-forth across the stage. She'd zoomed in as tightly as she could so that each of the seven figures and their captors were retained in focus in the center of the frame of her vision.

"That's better. Let the end game begin."

The man walked to the end of the line where a woman with thick fiber-optic tendrils flowing from her head instead of hair stood struggling between two masked figures. The woman stared wide-eyed as the leader approached her with the metal tube in his hand.

"The only solution we have is to make these people human again. The only solution we have is to give them back their humanity if only in the last moments of their misguided lives."

Cass understood what was about to happen now. Horror filled her. A scream sounded in her ears, one she only later realized was her own.

"No!"

The leader jabbed the tube against the metal implant in the side of the woman's head. The silvery, fiberoptic tendrils of cyber-hair stood straight out from her head for an instant as the electrical charge from the powerful battery pack on the men's belt fired into her implant frying the electronics and circuits inside.

"Be human again and be saved," the man shouted over his microphone as the powerful electric jolt destroyed the woman's brain along with the electronics in the implants. Her body spasmed and collapsed to the stage as the people on either side of her let go.

Cass screamed again. "No!"

Next to her, watching on the tablet, Shelby sobbed and muttered, "No, no, no," as the man continued down the line to the next person.

The second cyber-human struggled violently against the hold of his captors, but he could not break free. Once again, the man in the mask jabbed that metal tube against the man's implanted cerebral control center.

Once again, the body spasmed and fell lifeless to the stage. Cass watched, tears streaming from her one human eye as she watched and recorded what happened. The third cyber-human was killed just like the first two.

Eric was next.

He was still weak from his stay in the hospital and his struggles looked feeble and completely ineffective as the two muscular figures on either side held him while the man with the tube approached.

Shelby screamed. She dropped her tablet and ran to the edge of the rooftop. "Eric, no!"

It was too late. In a split second, as the tube tapped against the side of Eric's implant, he was gone.

Cass froze. She could not record this any longer. She wanted more than anything to stop, but she couldn't look away. Eric lay in a heap on the stage as the man continued down the line, finishing off the other three captives. The crowd cheered for each death, applauded each kill. When the seven people lay dead on the stage, the masked leader slid the tube back into the pouch on his belt and raised his hands over his head until the crowd fell silent.

"This is the only acceptable solution for anyone who considers themselves a human being. We, the members of Sapiens First, are your front-line defenders. We're here to protect you from the horror that is the Mantle AI's attempt to take over the world. Fight back or die."

With that final statement, the masked man placed the microphone back in the clip on the stand at the center of the stage. He turned with his followers and left the stage, blending back into the crowd. Other masked people came up and dragged the seven limp bodies offstage as well.

Cass could no longer watch. She cut the connection and slumped down to the rooftop, her back resting against the brick parapet. Shelby sobbed next to her, rocking back-and-forth with her knees hugged to her chest, calling out her brother's name.

Cass's mind spun with questions. Was this what her parents had meant when they referred to the end game? How could they condone such brutality? Cass wanted to ask her parents the question directly, although a small voice in the back of her mind told her she already knew the answer.

A chime pinged her implant, followed by another, and another, and another. She looked at the incoming messages. They were all from local and national net newsfeeds.

Cass checked the pings as a matter of course and gasped.

All over the country, the video Shelby streamed from her tablet was being picked up and reported on by news organizations across the country.

The videos played on the news feeds over and over again. The deaths of the seven people on that stage were witnessed again and again, as millions tuned in to watch the horrible display as it replayed countless times.

Cass sobbed and turned off her connection to the Mantle. She didn't want additional alerts of its viewing. She didn't need to see the video recording, she'd never forget the images as long as she lived.

Chapter 26

THE TWO WOMEN huddled together on the rooftop for a long time, crouched down behind the parapet in fear they might be found or seen if they tried to leave their hiding place. What would stop the same thing from happening to them?

While they remained hidden, they reopened their Mantle connection and watched as the news media carried the video of the deaths on all the channels.

The reporters and experts talked about how the Sapiens leadership were implicated in the deaths witnessed in the recording. Some others, friendly to the movement, proposed it was a staged event and the people weren't really dead. It was all an act.

Cass pulled Shelby close and hugged her tight. Shelby's sobbing continued unabated, her face pressed against Cass's shoulder.

"Shel, we need to get out of here. I know it's going to be risky to exit the building right now with all the Sapiens demonstrators down there, but I'm afraid if we stay here we're going to be discovered."

"So what?" Shelby asked. "I don't want to go down there. Call the police we saw earlier to come up and get us."

"Shelby, you saw what happened. We have to help ourselves. I don't know where the police were while Eric died, but we can't count on them helping us out of this."

"What are we going to do then?"

"I don't know, we need to get back to the dorm. It'll be safe on campus. Then we can make some decisions about what to do next. Maybe the video we recorded can be used as evidence in some way to identify who those people were in the black masks."

Cass started to say more, then froze as voices sounded from across the rooftop.

A man shouted at them, "You two, stay where you are. I want to talk to you."

Cass spun around and saw a man marching towards them across the flat gravel rooftop. He wore a red Sapiens rally shirt and he pointed as he approached with a snarl on his face.

"I figured out where that video came from," he said, waving his phone at them. "I knew it had to be from over here somewhere. It was you two, wasn't it?"

"I don't know what you're talking about," Cass said. "Stay away from us. We're not hurting anybody up here."

"You're coming with me. Both of you. I think you need to speak to some of my friends. If you come along peacefully, you won't be hurt."

"How can you say that?" Shelby shouted. "You people killed my brother while the rest of them stood there and watched like it was some holovid drama. You killed him and nothing is going to change that. Our video is the evidence that proves that your so-called movement is nothing but a smokescreen for a bunch of animals."

The wicked smile playing across the man's face told Cass he'd just gotten the proof he needed. He now knew it was their video playing everywhere. He slowed as he advanced, hands outstretched to grab at them.

Cass tugged at Shelby's arm, pulling her to her feet. "Come on. We've got to get out of here."

"You're not going anywhere," the man shouted as he reached out for Cass's arm. "I'm taking you in so we can make an example out of you, too. If we can get the original footage, we can make people believe it was all faked by your precious AI."

Cass yanked her arm out of the man's grasp. She reached out and shoved him with her free hand. "Let go of me. We're not going anywhere with you."

Her desperate shove caught the man off balance and he stumbled backward.

His eyes widened as the back of his knees hit the low brick parapet of the rooftop.

For one horrible instant, his arms wind-milled, trying unsuccessfully to regain his balance as he teetered on the edge. Cass thought for a brief moment about reaching out to grab hold of him and pull him to safety. Something inside her stopped her hand midway there.

The helpless man reached out for her, his fingers inches from hers, then he toppled backward, disappearing over the edge of the roof.

She didn't hear him yell or make any other sound. For a moment Cass wondered if he'd survived the fall somehow or maybe caught himself.

She ran forward and peered over the edge. The man lay in a crumpled heap on the sidewalk below, a pool of blood spreading outward on the pavement around his head.

"Oh my God, Cass," Shelby said, now standing next to her. "You killed him."

"Did I? I had no choice. It was an accident. He pulled at me and I just pushed him away."

"We need to get out of here," Shelby said. "We have to leave, now. When they find his body, they're going to come up here to see what happened."

Cass's mind filled with a mix of emotions. Her sense of right and wrong waged war within her over what she'd done. She knew it was an accident and believed in her heart she could explain it to the authorities when the time came.

Another part of her wondered if the authorities would even listen to her given that she was part of the counter-march and had recorded that damning video. It didn't show the city police in a good light as they stood by and did nothing.

Shelby pulled her arm. "Come on, Cass. We have to get down from here before someone shows up and starts looking for how he fell."

Cass stumbled along the rooftop, her feet shuffling through the gravel as Shelby pulled her towards the stairwell door in the center of the flat roof. The door was unlocked and together they ran down the stairwell inside the building.

When they reached the ground floor hallway and started towards the front of the building, they saw people in the street outside where the body lay. Some of them pointed upward.

Shelby and Cass stayed back from the window by the front door. Shelby pointed towards the rear of the building. "Let's head out the back and see if we can cross over to the next building behind us. We can get out that way onto the next street over. Come on."

Cass moved like she was on autopilot. Her mind filled with excuses for what she'd done. Guilt over the man's death wracked her.

Shelby tugged at her arm again and Cass nodded, following along behind Shelby as she led her by the hand.

They ran out the rear of the building into an alley. There were dumpsters along one side and across from them was another similar brick building like the one they'd exited. Shelby ran across the alley and pulled at the steel door there. She smiled when it popped open.

"Come on Cass, in here."

Cass followed as Shelby darted inside. The instant the door shut behind them, Cass heard shouts from the alleyway behind them. For a second, she was sure they'd been seen.

Shelby slid a metal bolt across into the door's steel frame, locking it. They crouched by the door for a few seconds, trying to get their wits about them and figure out which way to go next. As they did, multiple voices of people running by outside drifted in to them.

"He fell from up there."

"Did anyone see what happened?"

"What was he doing up there?"

"I thought I saw two people up there with him."

"He said something about knowing where the video came from. Maybe he thought there was a camera up there."

The voices receded down the alley as the people ran around the corner towards the side of the building with the fire escape. Cass and Shelby stood up and looked out the small basement window beside the door. The alley was now empty.

Shelby pointed to the other side of the room.

"There are the stairs up to the main floor. Come on Cass."

Once again, Shelby tugged Cass with her, heading towards the stairs up to the building's first floor. They ended up in the entrance hallway with apartments off to either side all the way to the front of the building.

Cass no longer needed Shelby's prodding to keep moving. They paused only long enough to look both ways out the front door for any sign of protesters. Seeing none, Cass opened it and she and Shelby headed out to the street.

Shelby must've already called an auto cab on her implant. One came up the street, homing in on her GPS location. The driverless car pulled to a stop right in front of the building as they reached the sidewalk.

"Get in, Cass. Hurry up. Let's get out of here."

Cass slid into the back seat. Shelby jumped in beside her and pulled the door shut. The cab pulled out into the street and drove away. It passed right by the square in front of City Hall.

Demonstrators milled around in front of the stage listening to the next speaker on the day's agenda. They acted as if nothing had happened.

Cass wondered where they'd dragged Eric's body to as the whole, strange scene passed by.

Shelby must've been thinking about the same thing. "What are they going to do with his body, Cassie? We can't go get him. What will they do with him?"

Cass didn't have an answer. She couldn't think about anything but the horrible vision of that man falling to his death. She saw him reaching for her partially outstretched hand, the hand she'd pulled back to protect herself.

Twenty minutes later, the auto cab pulled up at the edge of campus. Shelby and Cass climbed out, standing on the sidewalk in front of their dorm. They stood there for many long seconds just staring at the building as dusk fell around them.

After a long wait in the approaching darkness, Cass took a step towards the front door. She reached out and held Shelby's hand, pulling her girlfriend along with her as they returned to their room. Cass didn't know about Shelby, but her mind was in a daze on the walk to their room.

Chapter 27

THE TWO OF them didn't talk at all on their return to the room. The day's events had exhausted them. They ended up falling asleep in each other's arms after only a few minutes in their bed.

Cass woke up with a start hours later and checked the time. It was 5:30 AM.

Shelby stood over by her dresser. Cass lifted herself up on one elbow in her bed trying to figure out what her girlfriend was up to.

"Shelby, what are you doing?"

"I'm packing."

That caught Cass's attention. She sat all the way up in bed.

"Packing, what do you mean you're packing? Where are you going?"

"Don't make this harder than it has to be, Cass. I need to be with my family right now. My mother called me. They saw the video. She and Dad are devastated, as you can imagine. They didn't find out from the authorities like they should have. They heard from another family member who saw the video and sent them the link. Mom sent me a message an hour ago."

"What did she say?"

"She wanted to make sure I was all right. She doesn't think it's safe for me here and she wants me to come home for a while until things settle down."

"So, you're just leaving me? Now, after all of what happened yesterday?"

Shelby turned around to meet Cass's eyes. Redness rimmed the edges of her eyes from crying. "Don't make me do this the hard way, Cass."

"What do you mean? Packing to leave while I'm asleep isn't the 'hard way?' I think there are easier ways to tell me you're leaving."

"I think we need to take a little bit of a break, Cassie. I can't be here for you and home for my family at the same time. My mom and dad need me right now, don't you understand that?"

Cass didn't respond. She was still sort of asleep and all of this confused her. "What about your classes? If you leave school now, you'll fail out of your first semester."

"I sent messages to my professors explaining there was a sudden death in the family. Hopefully, once they find out what happened, they'll allow me to make up the work later or do it from home. Either way, family is more important than staying here at school."

"But you have me here for you," Cass said, trying to convince Shelby to stay. "Don't you understand that we need each other, now, more than ever? How am I going to come up with a plan to go home at the end of the semester without your help? My family is going to disown me when they find out about my implant. I'll never hide it from them the entire time I'm away on break. I don't know what they'll do to me."

Shelby shook her head. "Cass, your dad doesn't like me very much, but I can't see him doing something like what they did to my brother just because you've had medical implants. He might be pissed about it, but he'll find a way around his feelings."

Cass heard the words, but she wasn't sure. There was also the problem of her being a murderer now. As she thought about it, the shocked face of the man just before he toppled over the edge of the roof flashed into her mind again.

She shook her head to clear it and walked over to Shelby.

"Will I be able to see you after you go home? I could get a train up to your parent's place in Boston to visit. I haven't met your parents yet."

Shelby shrugged. "We'll see. A lot is going on right now and I don't want to overwhelm them with somebody new."

"So that's it?" Cass asked. "We're just through because all of this happened. This is when we need to be together even more. Don't you see that?"

"Cass, you have to stop. I had to make a decision. Right now, I have to be with my parents. It's not that I don't love you anymore. I do. It's that I need to be somewhere else right now and can't give you the attention you need."

"So, I'm on my own."

"Don't say it like that. Just give me some time. You finish out the school year. I'll reach out to you when I get back home. I'll help you plan for the semester break. I promise."

"Really?"

"You've got that skin patch if you decide not to tell your parents. That should keep them from noticing anything. Your hair will finish growing back by then. Just be careful, take it one step at a time and you'll be fine. Hopefully, I'll figure a way to come back next semester after I get things settled at home. Then we can start over again."

Shelby turned back to her dresser and continued placing her clothes in her bag.

Cass turned away and went over to sit on her bed. She had nothing more to say. How could Shelby abandon her at a time like this? Cass knew she'd promised to keep in touch with her, but it wasn't the same as having Shelby here.

Cass sat in silence with her back to the room as Shelby finished packing up her clothes and grabbing a few personal items from her desk.

She walked around to stand in front of Cass. "I'll be back to get the rest of the things later. Maybe it's best if I let you know when that will be so we don't have to see each other."

"You're leaving now? It's not even six in the morning."

"Mom and Dad caught the overnight train into the city. They

need to go down and identify Eric's body at the morgue when it opens. I'm going to go with them. They already arranged a ticket for me on the noon train back up to Boston with them."

It was all happening so fast and Cass's mind flipped through questions and angry retorts that she wanted to throw at Shelby. In the end, she stood and pulled Shelby close in a tight hug. Cass never wanted to let her go, but at least they'd leave on good terms.

Shelby took a step back and leaned forward to plant a soft kiss on Cass's lips. It was a moment of peace in the midst of the chaos of the last twenty-four hours.

Then it was over.

Shelby sighed and stepped back. "Bye, Cassie. I'll check in with you when I get to Boston. Good luck on your final. You'll do great."

Cass didn't say anything. She tried a half smile and nodded, not trusting herself to speak at that moment.

Shelby smiled back at her and turned to leave. Cass watched her go until the door swung shut behind her.

She stood all alone in the place that had become her sanctuary, at least as long as Shelby was there by her side. Now she had to figure out the next chapter of her life all by herself. Between finals, seeing her parents again, and trying to live a lie at home, Cass had a lot to do if she was going to make it through the next few months.

Like the story? *Leave a Review.*

Cass Armstrong's story continues with
Cyber's Escape - book 2
coming soon.

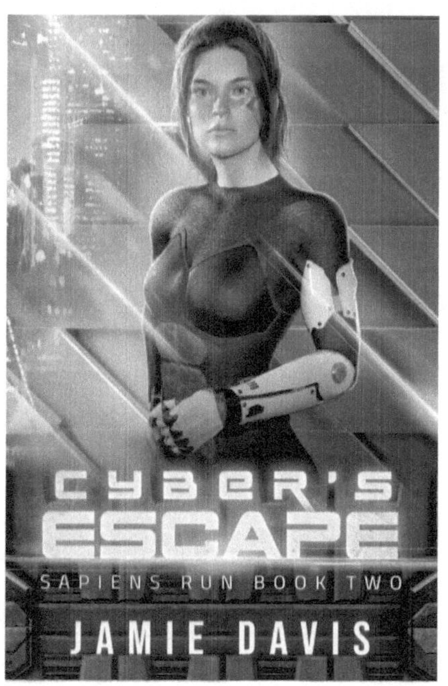
CYBER'S
ESCAPE
SAPIENS RUN BOOK TWO
JAMIE DAVIS

Afterword

A note from the author -

Those of you who've read a lot of my other books might notice this one is a little bit different from my usual fare. I actually had the idea for this story rattling around in my head for a few years. It stems from a time when I was a journalist covering medical technology and the concept of using cybernetics to improve the lives of humans intrigued me. The ethical implications did as well.

As I started writing fiction a few years later and I thought about the future from time to time, my earlier thoughts on cybernetics came back to me. Those thoughts began to take shape into a story about the ethical and social concerns that might accompany a world with cybernetic implants and augmentation. I'd ponder the idea now and then over the next few years, then I'd put it away and let it percolate for a while in the background as I wrote other things.

About a year before I wrote *Cyber's Change*, my youngest daughter challenged me to add more diverse characters to my books. Part of the challenge she set before me was to make their diversity "there" but not the reason for the story. As she told me based on the books she'd read, many authors wrote stories about gay couples where everything in the story was about their orientation. She proposed I write a story where they were just a couple like any other.

Challenge accepted!

Not long after that conversation, I was finally ready to begin a new series project and got started tackling the Sapiens Run trilogy starting with *Cyber's Change*. I dug in as I always do — with the main character.

As I created the character of Cass Armstrong, I realized she needed a love interest. To get through everything she had to face in her life after the accident, Cass would need a soulmate to pull her back to the surface when she was overwhelmed by the forces arrayed against her (from within and without). They could be male or female, but they had to love her with their whole being.

So, Cass and Shelby are just another couple. Yes, they happen to be gay, but in this world of the near future, there is no stigma associated with that. It just is. Instead, the drama and story action comes from elsewhere.

Cass and Shelby could just as easily be Cass and James. What mattered most was that they loved, argued, laughed, and cried together just like every other couple in the world. In the end, it was only important that they be there for each other when it mattered most.

To my daughter and her fiancé, I hope I've achieved the task set before me. I modeled Cass and Shelby not just after the two of you but also after my own early relationship with Mom. All couples face similar challenges as their bonds stretch and grow, no matter who you are. In the end, as Cass learns beside Shelby, we're all human.

—

Eldara Sister Series (2 books)

Read book 1 - *The Nightingale's Angel*

—

Follow on Facebook for updates, news, and upcoming book excerpts

Facebook.com/jamiedavisbooks

—

I Need Your Help ...

Without reviews indie books like this one are almost impossible to market.

Leaving a review will only take a minute — it doesn't have to be long or involved, just a sentence or two that tells people what you liked about the book, to help other readers know why they might like it, too. It also helps us write more of what you love.

The truth is, VERY few readers leave reviews. Please help us out by being the exception.

Thank you in advance!

Jamie Davis

About the Author

Jamie Davis is a nurse, retired paramedic, author, and nationally recognized medical educator who began teaching new emergency responders as a training officer for his local EMS program. He loves everything fantasy and sci-fi and especially the places where stories intersect with his love of medicine or gaming.

Jamie lives in a home in the woods in Maryland with his wife, three children, and dog.

He loves hearing from readers and going to cons and events where he meets up with fans. Reach out and say "hi." Visit Jamie-DavisBooks.com for more books, free offers and more!

Follow Jamie Online
www.jamiedavisbooks.com